PRAISE FOR THE D

Here are some of the over 100,000 five star reviews left for the Dead Cold Mystery series.

"Rex Stout and Michael Connelly have spawned a protege."

AMAZON REVIEW

"So begins one damned fine read."

AMAZON REVIEW

"Mystery that's more brain than brawn."

AMAZON REVIEW

"I read so many of this genre...and ever so often I strike gold!"

AMAZON REVIEW

"This book is filled with action, intrigue, espionage, and everything else lovers of a good thriller want."

AMAZON REVIEW

COLD BLOOD

A DEAD COLD MYSTERY

BLAKE BANNER

RIGHTHOUSE

Copyright © 2024 by Right House

All rights reserved.

The characters and events portrayed in this ebook are fictitious. Any similarity to real persons, living or dead, is coincidental and not intended by the author.

No part of this book may be reproduced in any form or by any electronic or mechanical means, including information storage and retrieval systems, without written permission from the author, except for the use of brief quotations in a book review.

ISBN-13: 978-1-63696-160-6

ISBN-10: 1-63696-160-6

Cover design by: Damonza

Printed in the United States of America

www.righthouse.com

www.instagram.com/righthousebooks

www.facebook.com/righthousebooks

twitter.com/righthousebooks

DEAD COLD MYSTERY SERIES
An Ace and a Pair (Book 1)
Two Bare Arms (Book 2)
Garden of the Damned (Book 3)
Let Us Prey (Book 4)
The Sins of the Father (Book 5)
Strange and Sinister Path (Book 6)
The Heart to Kill (Book 7)
Unnatural Murder (Book 8)
Fire from Heaven (Book 9)
To Kill Upon A Kiss (Book 10)
Murder Most Scottish (Book 11)
The Butcher of Whitechapel (Book 12)
Little Dead Riding Hood (Book 13)
Trick or Treat (Book 14)
Blood Into Wine (Book 15)
Jack In The Box (Book 16)
The Fall Moon (Book 17)
Blood In Babylon (Book 18)
Death In Dexter (Book 19)
Mustang Sally (Book 20)
A Christmas Killing (Book 21)
Mommy's Little Killer (Book 22)
Bleed Out (Book 23)

Dead and Buried (Book 24)
In Hot Blood (Book 25)
Fallen Angels (Book 26)
Knife Edge (Book 27)
Along Came A Spider (Book 28)
Cold Blood (Book 29)
Curtain Call (Book 30)

ONE

It was raining. It was always raining. At least, that was the way it felt.

Through the windshield, I watched the crime scene officers in their white plastic suits, hunched, carrying their equipment from their van into the ugly redbrick building on Chatterton Avenue. The red lights from the patrol cars and the ambulance pulsed in an oddly lazy rhythm on the wet walls, and reflected, broken, in the puddles on the sidewalk and the blacktop.

It was three in the morning on the first of May.

"May Day." Dehan looked at me. In the slow pulsing red light, the shadows of raindrops trickled down her face. "Sucks," she said.

I sighed and nodded and pushed open the door of my ancient car. She got out the passenger side, and we hunched against the rain and moved inside the building at a run. The uniform on the door jerked his chin in greeting and said, "Top floor, Detectives. No elevator."

It was two flights to the second floor, but right away we were aware of the acrid smell. An officer watched us climb the stairs and flicked her eyes at the open door. "Detective Romano's in the living room. It ain't pretty."

Dehan followed me in. Mike Romano was standing just inside. Beside him was Frank, the ME. One of the crime scene guys was taking photographs. There was an old sofa on the right and a chair in front of a window made black by the glare of the overhead bulb. But the first thing you noticed was the thick black smears on the ceiling and on the walls and the lingering traces of smoke.

On the floor, between the TV and the sofa, there was something that had once been a woman. Her face, waxy gray, was shaped by terror: Her eyes were staring, her mouth gaped, but her expression was empty because there was no life left there. The life had gone. Her abdomen was open, cut in an L from her lower belly to her ribcage. The carpet was saturated with half-congealed blood. Bloody footprints moved away toward the bedroom and the bathroom. Dehan said quietly, "Size nine."

Romano turned to look at us and spoke around his chewing gum. "There ain't nothin' here for you. What do you want?"

I took my time examining his face. "Do I need to explain myself to you, Mike?"

"Yeah, you do. This is my crime scene. You're treading on evidence. What do you want?"

I looked away at the body and spoke quietly. "It's the 43rd's crime scene, Romano, and the chief asked me to come and have a look. He'd like you to be cooperative." I offered him a pleasant smile. "You know how to be cooperative, don't you, Romano? You put your lips together and blow. You want to call him and have him explain it to you? You might just catch him before he gets back to sleep." I pointed at the body. "Who is she?"

He swore under his breath before muttering, "Elaine Gallardo. You can read all about it in my report."

I transferred my gaze to Frank. "What are we looking at? Is it him?"

He gave me a look that was skeptical. "The Castle Hill Ripper? It's too soon to say, John. I haven't had a good look at the body yet. I'll be able to tell you something when I've made an initial examination."

There was a flash, and the photographer nodded at Frank.

"I'm done, Doc. Go ahead."

Frank moved to the body and hunkered down. Dehan pointed at the footprints and spoke to Mike. "Where do the prints lead?"

"Bedroom and en suite."

"Scene of crime done in there?"

"Yah, whatever, just don't tread on anything."

"Yeah, if you like, I'll make like a fairy and float." She squeezed past the sofa to avoid the blood on the carpet. "Is that what you do, Mike, float like a fairy?"

There was some suppressed chuckling as I followed her through the bedroom to the en suite. By the time they got there, the prints had worn off most of the blood. Joe peered out of the bathroom in his white plastic suit.

"I thought you two might show up."

"It's the thought of you in that white plastic, Joe. I never can resist it."

He gave a small laugh. "Yeah, my wife has the same problem. You're wondering if he took a shower, right?"

It was Dehan who answered. "That, and what's with the damn smoke?"

"Looks like she was boiling some eggs when she was killed. They boiled dry, then the eggs began to burn. Eggs make a lot of smoke."

"You're not kidding. Did he? Take a shower?"

"It's looking that way."

"Son of a gun." She pointed back at the prints by the bedroom door. "He had plastic bags over his shoes, right?"

Joe nodded. "Yup. And I'll be able to tell you more when we've got this stuff back to the lab, but from the stains on the floor, it looks like he changed his clothes in here, too."

I said, "Thanks, Joe. Send me a copy of the report when it's ready, will you?"

"You got it."

We made our way back to the living room. Mike was leaning on the doorjamb with an unlit cigarette in his mouth. Outside, I could hear a gurney bumping up the stairs. We joined Mike by the door, and Frank looked up.

"Obviously, I need to prepare a full report, but on the face of it, the wounds to the belly—the disemboweling—were either pre-mortem or perimortem, and therefore probably the cause of death. That is indicated by the amount of blood, which tells us the heart was beating when the injuries were inflicted, and the expression on the poor woman's face. I can tell you no more than that at this stage."

Dehan said, "Frank, was she pregnant?"

He took a deep breath and sighed noisily. "How did I know you were going to ask me that? I don't know, Carmen. I need to get her back to the lab." He hesitated. "It's possible, but don't quote me, and please allow me to confirm it."

"You'll send us a copy of the report?"

"Of course."

Mike gave her the onceover, then me. I asked him, "You got her cell? Do we know who she's been talking to?"

"No. No cell. Looks like the killer took it. I thought they'd retired you to cold cases. The only thing cold here is that woman in there."

"Yeah, Mike, you be sure to explain that to the chief back at the station house. I'm sure he'll be grateful for your insight."

We stepped back to let the gurney through. As we made our way down the stairs, Mike came out and stood leaning on the banisters watching us.

"You know you're a real asshole, Stone," he called after me. "Don't forget to invite me to your retirement party. That's something I don't wanna miss."

Dehan laughed. "Take it easy, Tinker Bell."

He flapped a big hand at us, made an ugly noise, and withdrew, muttering obscenities.

We hunched back through the rain, clambered into my old burgundy Jag, and slammed the doors. Dehan said, "Station house?"

I turned the key in the ignition and made the big engine roar. "Where else would you want to be at three-twenty on a Monday morning when it's raining?"

By the time we got to Fteley Avenue, and I pulled in to park the rain had eased to a drizzle, and the first hints of gray were touching the eastern horizon, though dawn was still a couple of hours away. I gestured with my chin at a large Charger beside us. "The chief's here. That's his car."

Dehan nodded. "He's not a happy man. I can't say I blame him. This does not feel good."

The wet blacktop gave our steps a damp echo as we crossed the road. We climbed the stairs, grabbed three cups of black, tasteless water from the coffee machine, and while I carried them, Dehan knocked on his door.

"*Come!*"

She pushed in, and he watched us with anxious eyes. "Good! John, Carmen, I am very glad to see you. You've been to Chatterton Avenue?"

I placed a coffee on his desk, and we sat.

"We've just come from there. Frank says she might have been pregnant. Joe says he might have showered and changed his clothes after killing her. It was an L-shaped cut, from her lower belly up to her ribcage on her left-hand side. So taking in the intestines and the womb but not the liver. There were bloody footprints from the scene of the killing to the bathroom. Size nines. He had plastic bags on his feet, so he left no impressions of his soles. Frank and Joe will both send us copies of their reports. Mike Romano is pissed and wants me to invite him to my retirement party."

The chief sagged back into his chair. "I feared this. You both know I did. I was not happy with the conviction."

Dehan cleared her throat and spoke my thoughts.

"Sir, is this a cold case? The Castle Hill Ripper is officially in prison. That case is closed. This could be a copycat. I am pretty sure that's the line Mike is going to take. We would need more than a similar murder to reopen that investigation." She gave a small shrug and shook her head. "David Clark confessed to those killings. This is a hot case, not a cold one."

"I know." He ran his fingers through his tightly curled hair and repeated with more emphasis, "I know!" Then he sat chewing his lip and giving his head tiny shakes as he stared at the wall. "But I was never *satisfied*, Carmen. I told the DA I wasn't satisfied. But he and Mike were convinced. And when Clark confessed, that was it. Case closed."

I was frowning. "What are you thinking? Are you going to take the case away from Romano and give it to us? Do that and he'll be after my funeral, not my retirement."

"No, I can't do that. The fallout would be too great, and the pressure on you would be too much. No, Detective Romano will investigate this murder, as he did the Ripper murders. I will have him report to me daily, and the moment it seems credible that Dave Clark's conviction was unjust, I will take action." He wagged his finger in the air. "But at the same time, I want you, *discreetly*, to look into those original murders. Review them and the original investigation. I am far from convinced that Dave Clark is guilty. I think he is a deeply troubled man who needs help, but he did not kill those women."

I arched an eyebrow at him. "So this is a parallel investigation to Romano's?"

"Yes."

"Is it official or unofficial?"

"It is an official investigation. I want to know if the original conviction was just. And that is what you are officially looking into. How you go about it is your business, but I'd like you to keep me updated."

"Sure." I looked at Dehan. "So we'll pull the file and start going through it."

I stood, but Dehan remained sitting. "Sir, Mike is going to be a pain in the ass—"

"Unlike other detectives who spring to mind," he said with a smile.

"Sir, with respect, I am a major pain in the ass for a lot of people. But with me, the case always comes first, and when I have to, I cooperate. Mike is not in the mood to cooperate. So what I am asking is, will you make it clear to him that he is *required* to cooperate with us?"

"Yes, Carmen, I'll do that. But I would also like the two investigations to cross over as little as possible."

He reached over to the end of his desk and grabbed a thick manila file which he hefted over and dropped in front of her.

"I had it sent up," he said. "The original and a copy. Try to focus as much as you can on those six murders. I want the weaknesses in the original evidence so we can shoehorn them into this case."

She nodded and stood. I grabbed the file, and we left with our coffee.

Downstairs in the detectives' room, she dropped into her chair, and I dumped one of the two files in front of her before lowering myself into my own seat. I took a pull on the tepid, coffee-like liquid in the cup and started a general overview. After some fifteen minutes, Dehan started talking.

"Is this the first sign of a pattern? The first two murders were in 2018, about six months apart, May and November, Sandra Gavilan and Tomasina Traubert. Then nothing for a year, no sign of him throughout 2019. In 2020, he kills again in May, Nompumelelo Moyo, and then again in November, Caren Mitchell. 2021, May, Angela Garcia and November, Maria Romero; and in December of that year Dave Clark is arrested, and there is nothing during 2022. Now, first of May 2023, Elaine Gallardo is murdered."

I had leafed to the page she was looking at and nodded. "It looks like the beginning of a pattern. May and November, two on, one off."

She started talking again.

"All six murders, now seven, were committed in the Castle Hill area, within an area bounded by Soundview Avenue in the west, Randall Avenue in the south, Castle Hill Avenue in the east, and the Bruckner Expressway in the north." She paused and looked up. "This one, Elaine Gallardo, spills over to the north side of the expressway by one street, so we can either say this is not the Castle Hill Ripper or, more likely, those confines were purely the product of opportunity, not his MO."

"That's where he operated, and his victims happened to live there."

"Exactly." She looked back at the file and continued. "The first victim: Sandra Gavilan, twenty-three years old, lived at 1815 Story Avenue." She looked up again. "This guy is cold. What is that, five hundred yards from the cop shop?" She continued reading, "She is found when a neighbor checks on her because she doesn't show for coffee. They were close, and the neighbor had a key."

She went quiet for a minute, and I leafed to the report of the arrest. As I was reading, Dehan started talking again.

"There was no sign of forced entry." She leaned back in her chair to look at me and repeated, "No sign of forced entry. She was lying in the middle of the floor, like Elaine. She had an L-shaped cut from lower belly to ribcage over the intestines and not the liver. She had been pregnant, and the killer had gone to the bathroom, showered, and changed his clothes. They were able to tell that because of the stains on the floor and, obviously, with that much blood on him, he would have been noticed in the street. He had wrapped plastic around his shoes so the tread of his soles could not be identified."

"So he knew in advance that he was going to walk across a blood-saturated floor to have a shower."

"This guy is cold. Real cold."

"If this is a copycat, the copycat is as cold as the original killer."

She narrowed her eyes. "How likely is that?"

"I don't know." I looked down and tapped the notes I was reading. "When Clark was arrested, they found in his garage a heavy-duty garden garbage bag with six plastic bags in it. Each bag contained a set of bloodstained clothes and a small notebook. The blood was a match for each of the girls, and the notebook recorded in great detail the process of choosing and identifying the victim, stalking her to acquire information about where she lived and what her daily habits were, whether she lived alone, who her friends were, et cetera. Apparently, he talked about them as though they were big game and he was a hunter. He referred to them as prey. All of them except the last shopped regularly at Shoprite, on the Bruckner Common, opposite where Kmart used to be. The last one, Maria Romero, actually worked there. Dave Clark had worked there in the storeroom and stocking shelves."

I paused to scratch my chin and think. We stared at each other for a moment. "Hence the geographical location of the victims. They were all customers at Shoprite—*including* Elaine Gallardo, who was killed last night."

She said, "Only..." and we both spoke at the same time. "Only Dave Clark doesn't work there anymore."

TWO

We spent another hour or so working through the other five cases: Tomasina Traubert on Homer Avenue, Nompumelelo Moyo on Lafayette, Caren Mitchell on Pugsley, Angela Garcia on Underhill, and Maria Romero on Olmstead. There was no substantial difference in the MOs. They were all killed at night. In each case, there had been no forced entry. The victims had apparently admitted the killer willingly and had then been killed pretty much in the middle of the living room floor. The method was disemboweling with an L-shaped cut from right to left across the lower abdomen and then up to the ribs, and in each case the women had been in the first few weeks of pregnancy.

The killer, having attacked the victims from the front, was presumably covered in a great deal of blood. In each case, he had walked to the bathroom, leaving footprints that suggested his feet were covered in plastic bags. There he had removed his clothes, showered, and dressed in fresh, clean clothes.

In each of the six, now seven, cases the police had been alerted by neighbors. Sometimes because a friend had noticed the victim's absence for some reason, as when Sandra Gavilan failed to show for coffee or because some kind of event or incident alerted them.

"It's always the neighbors who are alerted," I said. "Elaine Gallardo last night, it was because of the eggs."

She glanced at me over the file. "You think that's relevant?"

"Who knows? This guy has a peculiar way of thinking. These little notebooks, one for each victim, but he calls them prey. They are full of hunting terminology. He hunts pregnant women with a knife instead of a rifle."

She nodded absently more times than was strictly necessary while she read. Then she narrowed her eyes, shook her head, and sighed at the window. Outside the air was showing the first gray signs of a damp morning.

"Three details, the plastic bags to conceal the tread of his shoes, the showers with the change of clothes, and the hunting terminology. Those things were known only to the cops who investigated the case and to the killer. So if this is a copycat, it has to be either a cop who was involved in the original investigation or someone who knew the killer."

"Intimately."

"Intimately, yeah. To confide in him that he killed these women and how he did it, in detail, that's intimate."

"Either that or, as the chief suspects, they got the wrong guy, and the real killer is still at large."

She shook her head and made a face. "I don't buy that, Stone. I can't. The guy confessed. The only place where guys confess to murders they didn't commit is in Hollywood, in the movies."

I dropped the file on the desk. "Okay, we are basically familiarized with the case. The first step we need to take now is to go and talk to Dave Clark in Attica. You want to call and arrange it?"

She gestured at me with an open hand, then did a bit of Latin-cum-Mediterranean shrugging, hand spreading and head twitching.

"Mr. Macho Man makin' decisions here. Stand back. Give the man's ego some space. Do I get a say? Do I have an opinion?"

"No."

"Coz, you know, I was gonna say—"

"What?"

"We should go talk to him in Attica, form an opinion of the guy face to face. Get a feel for him. Know what I'm saying?"

"Come on, we'll get some real coffee and breakfast on the way."

She stood and grabbed her cell with one hand while shouldering on her black leather jacket with the other. "I'll ask the chief to call. They'll be more cooperative if he makes the arrangement."

He called back when we were on the River Parkway, passing the Botanical Gardens, to confirm they were expecting us around midday. We moved through the gloom of the yawning, stretching city, where windows winked on and sleepy citizens woke reluctantly to another Monday morning, fumbling their ways to their bathrooms, kitchens, and coffee pots. Trees and suburbs slipped by in the failing dark, spaghetti junctions, schools and gas stations, all slowly coming to life in the grainy dawn.

We didn't talk much, but when we'd crossed the river on the Mario Cuomo bridge and were cruising through Nyack on I-287, I spoke aloud the thoughts that were going around in my head.

"You said this guy is cold."

"He is cold."

"He is cold and brutal."

"Like a reptile."

"And yet, seven women allowed him into their houses at night. A pregnant woman, alone, in the Bronx, allows a man into her apartment at night. That is anomalous."

She nodded, gazing at the superabundance of trees passing by on our right. "So," she said after a moment, "either he is really skilled at befriending women and gaining their trust—"

"And that would have shown up in the investigation: one guy —the same guy—gaining the trust and friendship of each of these women."

"Or for some reason, he is not seen to pose a threat."

"Like?"

"Like a doctor, a security guard, a small defenseless woman…" She trailed off, paused, and finally said, "or a cop."

I laughed suddenly. "You're fantasizing! You want it to be Mike Romano, don't you?"

She laughed. "Yeah. Yeah, actually I do." Then, more seriously, "But that is two boxes ticked, right, Stone? Knowledge only the investigating officers knew and the fact that the women seemed to trust this guy. It could be a cop who was involved in the original investigation."

I grunted. "It's suggestive, yeah. But I kind of like the small, defenseless old woman angle. I think we should go with that."

The Attica Maximum Security Correctional Facility is just outside Attica the town and only fractionally smaller. It's about a mile long and a quarter of a mile across, and every time I go there I get the same eerie feeling, like I've stepped into one of those 1960s dystopian movies about a future where everybody is happy because nobody has a soul.

We parked in the lot, and fifteen minutes later we were shown into a secure interview room with concrete walls and no windows. A fluorescent strip on the ceiling gave a stark, dead light over a table and three chairs.

After another five minutes, the sound of steel doors echoed down a soulless passage, and a few moments after that, the door to the interview room clanged open and two uniformed guards led Dave Clark in. He was in his orange overalls. They sat him opposite us and handcuffed him to the table.

"You need us," one of them told me, "we're right outside."

I thanked them, and they left with another echoing clang of steel doors. I took a moment to study the man sitting opposite me. He was in his thirties. His eyes were dull, pale blue. Their expression was not one of resignation. They said they had never expected anything more than the brutish sordidness they had seen every day of his brutish life. He waited, without apparent interest or curiosity, looking first at me, then at Dehan.

He was strong, with a thick bull neck and a big jaw. His nose was broken, and his fists, resting on the table, were like two slabs of concrete. He wasn't ugly exactly, but he wasn't somebody you'd want your daughter to date.

"How's prison life, Dave?"

He shrugged. "It's okay. Better'n the streets."

After a moment, he gave a small laugh to let us know it had been a joke. I smiled.

"Less criminals, right?"

"Got that right."

"You made many friends?"

"Nah." He shook his head and looked oddly embarrassed. "I don't—" He stammered for a moment. "I don't, I, I—"

"You don't make friends a lot?"

"Nah."

"The other inmates give you a lot of trouble?"

"At first, y'know, coz they said I killed babies. But I told them, y'know, they weren't r-really pregnant. Like, you couldn't see it. The b-belly. And one guy, I broke his arm, and now I kind of do my own thing and nobody talks to me. I'm, it's, just me."

I wagged a finger at him and gave him a knowing smile, like me and him were sharing something.

"You're smart. I know—we know—you are smart." There was a ghost of a smile. "So I want to ask you something. You know the thing you did with the shoes?"

"I kind of remember. I put plastic bags over them and tied them, right?"

Dehan said, "You don't remember?"

"I don't remember a lot of things." He wasn't being a wiseass. He meant it. "My therapist says I'm suppressing memories I find intolerable to remember."

I nodded. "That's good that you're getting help. Who did you tell about the plastic bags over your shoes?"

He thought about it, looking down at his cuffed wrists. He thought about it so long I eventually asked him, "Can you remember? Can you remember anyone you told?"

"No."

Dehan leaned forward with her elbows on the table. "How about Detective Romano? Or some of the cops who were investigating the murders?"

"They found the notebooks." He stared at her for a long moment, then added, "And the forensic officers worked it out from the bloodstains. O-on the floor."

"How about friends?" I asked him. "Did you have a friend who you talked to about what you were doing?"

He was shaking his head. "I d-, I d-," He couldn't get passed the D, so he went for, "I never had…"

Dehan cut in, "You never had friends?"

"Never."

"Not even one special friend you told all your secrets to?"

"Never."

I asked him, "You like hunting, Dave?"

He shifted his gaze to the wall, like he thought there might be a window hidden there somewhere. "Yeah," he said.

"I've never hunted. I've thought about it. Would you recommend it?"

"Yeah."

"What is it you like about it? The fresh air, being in the wilds…?"

"No." He was still staring at the wall. "It's getting close, and they don't know. It's like secret, but you're getting so close sometimes you can touch them."

I smiled. "That's cool. I can imagine that's exciting. Did you used to do that in Shoprite? You were in the storeroom, right?"

"And loading shelves."

"Then you'd pick a pretty girl and see how close you could get, see if you could touch her?"

He shifted his eyes to the floor. He was frowning. The expression was one of suspicion. "Yeah…" he said.

Dehan asked him, "What about deer, moose, that kind of thing? Where did you hunt them?"

He raised his gaze to the ceiling, then slowly brought it down to my face. He answered me, not Dehan.

"I read about that."

"Oh, you never hunted big game?"

"No."

"You know anyone who hunts?"

"No."

I gave him a big smile. "Let me ask you something, because I have to say this really impressed me about you. I could never kill anyone. I'd be just too nervous. But you, not only did you perform the killing, after the hunt, but then you so calmly went to the bathroom, stripped off your clothes, had a shower, got dressed again…" I trailed off, shaking my head. "Were you not a nervous wreck while you were taking that shower?"

He was smiling. It was a sly smile, cautious. "No."

"I mean, somebody could have shown up at any moment. The cops could have shown up! You weren't nervous?"

His mouth was sagging slightly as he smiled and watched me. "No."

"That's amazing." I turned to Dehan. "Don't you think that's amazing?"

"I do. I wish I was that cool. Listen, Dave, there is something else I'd really like to understand. We all would, down at the station house." She leaned forward, shaking her head, awed. "How did you get them to let you in?" She laughed. His smile deepened. "I mean, what did you do? Bring them flowers?"

"Yeah, sometimes. They knew me from the store. Sometimes I'd take 'em shampoo or something from the shop. Something they needed. A-and I'd say, 'Hi, it's me, Dave, from the store. I brought you some shampoo…'" He trailed off.

I gave my head a single shake. "Smart."

Dehan said, "And then, once you're inside—"

"But I forget a lot." He cut across her, silencing her. "I forget. Dr. Cohen says I forget because I repress my m-memories, because I don't like who I was back then. I forget." He held her eye for a few seconds, then shifted his gaze to me. "I forget," he repeated. "I forget a lot."

I gave a small laugh, like we were just chatting over coffee. "Don't worry about it, Dave. It's all in the past, right? We just want to understand things a little better. If you help out, who knows? They might give you some privileges or something. So who was your favorite? Who gave you the biggest buzz?"

Again his eyes went astray, back to the ceiling, like he was watching things move up there that only he could see. "I don't…" He trailed off, then said, "I d-"

"Which one gave you the most excitement?"

"I don't remember." But then he smiled and said, "Maria." His eyes fixed on mine, still smiling. "Maria Romero, on the corner of Olmstead and Quimby. She was pretty." He gave Dehan a sidelong glance. "Black hair, brown eyes."

"She was your favorite?"

"Yeah."

Dehan asked, "Because she was pretty?"

His eyes sought the floor. "She was pretty."

I leaned back in my chair and crossed my arms. "What about Nompumelelo? Was she pretty?"

"I don't— She was—"

I waited. Eventually I asked him, "She was what?"

"She was—I don't remember. She was Black."

"Was she pretty?"

"No. I don't—"

"You remember Angela?"

He nodded. "M-hmm."

"Was she pretty?"

"Yeah."

"How about Sandra?"

"She was my first. She was pretty."

"So, Dave, how did you choose your—" I hesitated a moment, then went with, "How did you choose your girls?"

"I don't remember. They came to the store. Sometimes I

wanted to be close to them and touch them." He shifted his eyes to Dehan, but he still seemed to be talking to me. "I wanna go now. I don't remember anything else. I won't talk to you anymore."

I said, "That's okay, Dave. I'm done." I turned to Dehan. "You done?" She nodded, and we stood. "You want anything, Dave, you let me know."

But he was staring at the wall, looking for a window that wasn't there.

THREE

I leaned my back against the Jag and eyed the huge prison. It was like a bizarre mixture of a Bavarian castle and Disneyland. Dehan stood in front of me with her hands thrust in her pockets, going up and down on her toes, staring out at the lush green fields and woodland around us.

"I could say," she said, "with equal conviction, he is *definitely* the guy, or he is definitely *not* the guy."

I smiled and looked up at the very blue sky, reminding myself of Dave Clark looking up at the ceiling, apparently observing it in minute detail.

"He is definitely an interesting character."

She scowled at me. "You've made up your mind?"

I gave my head a single shake. "No. But I would observe that he is a very frightening man. He certainly gives the impression that he is not fully in control of his feelings, his actions, or his mind. And you're never quite sure what's going on in his mind." I gave a small shrug. "I guess that's why they had him in the storeroom and stocking shelves."

Her scowl softened to a frown. "He's all that."

"I'd also say he could probably use a few more seconds in the microwave."

"Really? Seriously? This is your improvement on a taco short of a combination?"

I ignored the comment. "And you're right. It is as easy to imagine he *is* the guy, as it is to imagine Romano *deciding* he's the guy and corralling him into a confession."

"Thank you. I think."

"There were times in there you just felt he wanted to check with someone what the right answer to a question was. Then he'd just clam up: 'I don't remember, I don't remember.'" I pointed at her. "You know what *you* need to clear your mind?"

"What? My mind is clear. What do I need?"

"A cold beer. I'll join you. The Prospector is good, on Main Street. We'll have lunch there. The smothered steak is especially good. You'll like it."

She climbed in the Jag beside me and slammed the door. "What if I don't?"

"Then I'll want to know what you've done with the real Dehan." I pulled out of the parking lot and turned right onto Exchange Street. "She's the kind of girl who enjoys a good smothered steak and a beer. My kind of girl."

She grinned and punched my shoulder. "Jerk!"

I smiled and pretended it didn't hurt.

We found a parking space on the bridge over the creek and walked the short distance to the restaurant. We sat at a table by the window and ordered two cold bottles of Bell's Two Hearted Ale and two plates of smothered steak.

The rain had stayed down on the coast. Here, gentle spring sunshine lay across the white linen tablecloth and highlighted the right side of Dehan's face. A single hair rising like an antenna from the top of her head gleamed and made me smile.

"What?" she asked with humor in her eyes.

"When I take early retirement and start writing my memoirs, I will record this moment."

She gave a small frown. "Why?"

"Because you are beautiful, and you lend the moment a beauty it would not otherwise have."

She blushed. "Wow, if I hadn't already married you, I'd marry you right now!" She was quiet for a moment, then, "Are you seriously thinking of retiring?"

I took a deep breath and looked out the large window at the Burgundy Beast, a 1964 Mk II, one of the most beautiful cars ever made. Worth preserving. Worth looking after.

"Cases like this one," I said. "They make me think. Where are my priorities? Have I got them lined up straight?" I looked her in the eye. "Are we going to have kids? If so, do we raise them in the Bronx? Do we continue working?"

She was frowning again, watching me carefully. "You haven't been thinking this since three a.m. this morning, Stone. How long has this been on your mind?"

I directed a small laugh at my fingers as I drummed them on the table. "Since before we got married. It was raining, we were in a narrow alley between Revere Avenue and Calhoun Avenue. As I recall, you were vomiting profusely, and I was getting very wet."[1]

"You retained all the relevant details, then."

"There isn't a detail of that day that isn't etched into my mind. But especially where I picked you up and you touched my face and told me you knew I'd come for you."

She grinned. "You're getting sentimental in your old age, pardner."

The waiter brought our beers and set them on the table. I thanked him, and as he went away, I said:

"I've always been sentimental, Dehan. You know that. It's just every day I see less reason to pretend I'm not. Look, back then, we put away Bob Luff, guilty of six murders and one attempted. And we didn't know it, but as he was going down, this guy, Dave Clark or whoever it is, was gearing up for his first kill. So if I was in my twenties or thirties, unattached and had only my Jaguar to think

---

1. See *Two Bare Arms*

about, I'd do my part. But to be honest, Dehan, at my age now, every time I look at you, I wonder if the risk is worth it."

She looked troubled. "So would you want me to stop working as a cop if you retired?"

I took a pull on my beer and smacked my lips. "That's the wrong question, Little Grasshopper. I have no right to ask you to change your chosen career, and I would never do that. But if you ask me would I be happy and relieved if you left the NYPD when I eventually retire and/or we have kids? Then that is a whole different ball game. Yes, I would. *Especially* if you were impregnated with the seed of life."

"This is kind of out of left field."

"Yup."

"Was it what that asshole said last night? Romano? He was looking forward to your retirement?"

"Maybe that got me thinking. I thought at the time I was probably looking forward to it more than he was."

"Couple of times I've thought I was pregnant, Stone."

"I know."

She shook her head. "We need to focus on the case, Sensei, but we need to talk about this too. This ain't something that's going to blow over."

"After the case. Let's take a drive up to Maine, Bath, or Sebasco. We'll walk barefoot on Popham Beach or Hunnewell and eat oysters and sirloin steak."

"And talk."

"And talk."

"You got yourself a deal, Stone."

The waiter reappeared with two generous helpings of smothered steak, and we ate in silence until the plates were clean. Then I leaned back and drained what was left of my beer and signaled the waiter for two more. To Dehan, I said,

"Back to business. All we've got are impressions. We have feelings and hunches based on the demeanor of a man who is either extremely stupid or extremely clever. So we have to note our impressions, recognize they are of limited use, and seek more substantial information. We need to start nailing down a few facts."

"Agreed. The sixty-four-thousand-dollar question is where the hell do we begin?"

"I'll tell you where I want to begin. I have no idea if it's feasible. It was five years ago, but I want to go and examine the original crime scene on Story Avenue."

"Sandra Gavilan's apartment?" She made a face that was dubious. "What for? It's probably been redecorated and inhabited since a week after her death."

"Maybe."

"Call me unimaginative, but wouldn't it be simpler to go and examine the current crime scene?"

"Yup, but the chief asked us not to tread on Mike's toes, and anyway, I want to see the *original* crime scene. This was his first kill, we assume. I want to imagine how he got there, in both senses, physically and mentally. What was he thinking? What did he say at the door? All that kind of dinosaur shit."

She pulled out her cell and made a call. She gazed out of the window for two rings, then said, "Sergeant Gonzalez, this is Detective Dehan—"

The waiter delivered two beers and went away. Dehan was saying, "...the new rookie, what's her name, Caroline? Caroline Gordon. Is she around? I need to talk to her last week... Yeah, would you? Thanks."

I raised my glass to her, and we drank. She said,

"Officer Gordon, this is Detective Dehan. I'm out of town right now, and I need you to do something urgently. I need you to find out who owns an apartment at 1815 Story Avenue." She gave her the exact address, then added, "Fastest route is just go there and ask. If that fails, then try ACRIS. It was the scene of a murder five years ago..." She looked at me and raised her eyebrows. "Oh you knew that already. Yes, the Castle Hill Ripper case, his first victim. That's correct. I want to see the property. So as soon as you have a name and a telephone number, let me know."

She hung up, picked up her glass, and drained it. "Six-hour drive back, Stone. We get there for seven or eight p.m. You want me to drive while you digest?"

I threw her the keys.

In the car, we pulled out of Attica and headed east and a little south toward home. Dehan was restless and kept making faces and sighing.

"It's the blueberry pie, right? You were in a hurry to leave, duty called, but man you wanted that blueberry pie! How much time would we have lost? Ten minutes, maybe fifteen? Was it worth it? Was it really worth the sacrifice?"

"You know me better than I know myself, Stone. We both know that, but that wasn't actually what was on my mind. I mean, I know we had to come. We had to see him and talk to him, know who we were dealing with. But hell. I can't help feeling we've just wasted twelve hours we could have spent doing something more useful."

I looked at her a little surprised. "You didn't find the visit useful? I did. I thought it was very useful."

She shrugged and shook her head. "For what?"

"For several things. Not least, everything we find out from now on, we will measure against the man we have just spoken to, and it will make sense, or it won't. You'll see what I mean when we visit Sandra Gavilan's apartment."

"You're such a jerk, Stone. You never share what you're thinking. You know already, don't you, whether it was Dave Clark or not. You do, don't you?"

"Off coss not, foorish child," I said in a passable Chinese accent. "Mind of mastah empty, like useful bit of window."

Then the smothered steak took over, and I slept for an hour while Dehan drove and fidgeted in her seat. I was awoken by her cell phone ringing. She thumped me on the shoulder and said, "It's Caroline Gordon, the rookie. You answer it."

I took the phone, put it on speaker, and levered myself upright in my seat.

"Hey, Caroline, this is Detective Stone. Detective Dehan is driving at the moment and can't multitask right now."

"Oh, okay. Hello, sir. So here goes. We're in luck. The apartment was sold after the murder of victim number one, Sandra Gavilan. It proved hard to sell because of the murder but was eventually bought, at a knock-down price, by a developer, the Bronx-Build Corporation. They went bust in 2021, and since then it has been sitting there gathering dust. Right now, it belongs to the Bank of Santander. I called their agent, and we can collect the key to view the place whenever suits you."

"That is sterling work, Gordon. Well done. Please go and get the key now. We'll see you when we get back, at about six-thirty."

"Thank you, Detective. I'll do that right away."

I hung up. Dehan said to the windshield, "Sterling work" with no particular inflection.

I arched an eyebrow at her and said, "Pfui, are you a dunce, madam?"

"Rex Stout now? I was always more of a Mickey Spillane gal. You know, 'I poked a Lucky in my mouth and went out to kill somebody.' You know what I mean?"

"I hear you. Again, I say pfui, madam."

We got back to the station house at six-fifteen, with the sun slipping and turning the air polished copper. While Dehan waited in the car, I stepped inside and collected the key from Officer Gordon, who had blue eyes and freckles.

"Is there any other way I can be of help, Detective Stone?"

"That's good work, Gordon. I'll keep you in mind."

"Thank you, sir. I'm ready."

Dehan was also ready. She covered the distance in a little less than thirty seconds, did a U-turn across double yellow lines, and parked in the bus lane.

"Lucky there are no cops around," she said, grabbing the file and a flashlight and climbing out. I followed. "If they tow it, you pay."

"If they tow it, I'll poke a Lucky in my mouth and go kill somebody. Come on, cowboy up."

I followed her past a sad lawn imprisoned behind rusty railings, under an ugly, covered area made sordid by depressing graffiti and bits of disowned garbage, to a steel elevator covered in obscene drawings, which we rode to the seventh floor. On the way up, Dehan pointed at the indelible black and red scrawls on the walls.

"We inhabit the same space, but we live in different worlds."

"That's deep."

"That was my dad. He was deep. I think of him often. He used to say two people can stand in the same place; one of them is in hell and the other in heaven."

The doors slid open, and we found the apartment at the end of a dim corridor. Halfway down, there was a large flowerpot. The earth was dry, and the plant was dead, but nobody had bothered to steal the pot.

I unlocked the door, and we went in.

FOUR

The first thing that hit you was the stench. It was a testament to the lack of interest a bank has in an unsellable product. A thing is worth what you can get for it. And what you can get is always measured in cash.

Then, aside from the smell, there was that special kind of darkness you get in filthy, musty spaces, like the darkness itself might be dirty.

Dehan muttered, "Jesus!" and I took a detour around the carpet and the low coffee table to pull back the drapes. Murky, late-afternoon light leaned in, with none of its copper sheen. Motes of dust hung suspended in the shafts of dull light, drifting slowly up and down, and where they formed a distorted, luminous oblong on the carpet, a large, ugly stain disfigured the beige pattern with matted blackness.

I pointed at Dehan's feet. She looked down at the dry spatter of bloodstains, took a step in, and turned to face the door. After a moment, she reached out and pushed it closed. The Yale latch clicked.

To her left, there was a small fold-down table. She opened it up and set the file there.

"Rosario Gomez, the neighbor, let herself in with a key. She was very clear about that. That means the door was closed." I nodded. She went on, pointing at the huge bloodstain, which was nine or ten feet in front of her. "So I'm the killer. I ring on the bell, Sandra comes to the door—" She turned and pointed to the peephole. "She looks, right? This is the Bronx, not Big Timber, Montana. She's not expecting Parson Johansen or Sheriff Seth O'Connell to come around for coffee and blueberry pie, right? So she looks through the peephole."

"Yes."

"Forgive me if I am going painfully slowly, but I want to get this clear. *Having seen who it is*, she opens the door."

"Right."

"She and her killer then wind up ten feet inside the room. That's like four or five steps." She took three long steps to the bloodstain. "Nine, ten feet." She then moved back to the door, pointing at it. "But the door is closed."

"Tell me why the door is closed. He might have closed it when he left, after he'd killed her."

"Because of the blood spatter. If the door had been open, it would have reached the door on both sides. It didn't. So it was closed."

"Okay."

"So that means he did not rush her."

"I agree, but tell me why."

She held up her index finger. "One, you can't rush somebody and close a door at the same time. If he had tried, she would either have attacked him and screamed or run and screamed. There were no reports of screams. Also, two"—she held up her middle finger—"this woman is pregnant and *really* protective of her baby. If she sees a knife, she is going to go crazy. She is going to alert the whole damned neighborhood. If he got ten feet into the room, and the door was closed, it's because she let him get that far. He didn't rush her."

I crossed the room, opened the door, and stepped out into the passage. There I closed the door and rang the bell. After a moment, I heard Dehan's voice.

"Who is it?"

The sixty-four-thousand-dollar question. What did she need to hear to let me in?

"It's me, from Shoprite. I've got your order."

There was a pause. Then she opened the door and held out her hand. "Thanks."

We stood there a moment looking at each other. "What do I need to do," I asked her, "for you to let me in and give me a glass of water?"

"On six different occasions, six different times, and six different women."

"Seven."

"Seven. I need to know you. And I need to trust you."

"Okay." I nodded. "So what are the chances that this guy is a trusted friend of all seven women and was *not* noticed by Mike Romano?"

"Nil."

"I agree, so we are back to trust. Which brings us back to a cop, a priest, or something of that nature."

"Yeah, and there is something else. A lot has been made of the fact that the victims were all close to Shoprite, and all frequented the store. But who doesn't around here? On the other hand, it is also true that all the victims lived within spitting distance of the 43rd Station House. Shoprite and the 43rd are less than half a mile apart."

"Good point. Another good point is one you made earlier."

"Right." She nodded. "I know. What?"

"In Big Timber, Montana, they probably trust the local lawman, the sheriff, or his deputy. He knocks on the door at ten or eleven at night, and they open the door to him without hesitation. But Story Avenue, in the Bronx? A lone cop knocks at your door at ten or eleven at night, is he somebody a Bronx resident would automatically trust?"

"No. And certainly not seven times in a row."

"Exactly. You are going to get very different reactions from different people. And there's something else. How is this cop coming into contact with these women? Shoprite offers that point of contact, but the copshop? We need to have a closer look at what—and *who*—these women have in common."

"Yeah, we should also look at their religious backgrounds. See if there is a minister or church they all had in common."

"Right, so, for the sake of the exercise, I am a smiling, trusted person. May I come in?"

She nodded. "Okay, so I am going to step back and to my left as I pull the door open, and say, 'Oh, hi! Come on in.'"

I took a step forward and said, "I won't close the door, you will. While you do, I will move forward to the middle of the floor, to the coffee table, and that will draw you after me. Which means either we are chatting, or I have brought something for you which I will set on the table, or for some reason we both take it for granted I am going to be here for a short while at least."

Dehan was frowning. "So hang on, Stone. If you go in ahead of me, how do I end up facing you with my back to the window? Because the blood spatter is toward the door."

We both stood, thinking, she behind me, me staring at the coffee table, the sofa, and the window. I said,

"Because I brought something for you. I am going to put it on the table, and you hurry over to clear a space. You straighten up to face me and zap."

"That is one hell of a lot of supposition, Stone."

"Yup, but right now, I am having a lot of trouble visualizing anything else. I'd lay money, whatever gets him through the door, gets him each time to the same position on the carpet. And it is the same in every case. Mike assumed it was a fetish of some kind. I think maybe it tells us how he gets in, and how he gets in is intimately tied up with who he is."

She frowned unhappily at me. "That s an inspirational leap."

"I know. I also know it's right. He brings something in. She closes the door, he waits by the coffee table, she hurries to make space, as she turns around, he stabs her in the lower belly—"

Dehan took up her position directly in front of me.

"He would have to step in close and hold her to stop her pulling away."

I put my left arm around her and closed in. "He makes the cut —the weapon must be exceptionally sharp—and then he lays her down on the floor."

"He is completely covered in blood."

"And so is the floor."

Dehan pointed at the folder. "In his report, Frank said the..." She hesitated. "The miscarriage..."

I nodded. "Yeah, I know. And that is obviously what he is after. This is the experience he needs to have. This is why he comes prepared with a change of clothes. When it's over, this is when he puts the plastic bags over his shoes." I shook my head. "He probably has them in whatever it is he places on the table. He puts them on and goes to the bathroom, where he showers and cleans himself. He is satiated, and he has no emotions at this point."

"Cold."

"Yes.

I turned and crossed the floor, following the faint stains that still remained. I heard Dehan behind me.

"Sweet Jesus, Stone, the owner, the developer, the bank, nobody thought it was worth cleaning this place?"

"Don't knock it; we may yet be grateful."

But the crime scene guys were nothing if not thorough, and they had found everything and anything that had been worth finding five years earlier. All that remained was the unwelcome possibility of standing in the bathroom where he had stood, on his bloody footprints, and realizing that he had gazed at himself in the mirror before stripping and showering. What had he seen in the glass? Who had he seen?

Dehan leaned on the doorjamb. We stared at each other in

silence for a moment. I said, "Size nine. It's not small, but it's slightly below average. He is small, unthreatening, and he is here in the bathroom taking the time to look at himself in the mirror, covered in gore."

She nodded absently. "He's not a cop, Stone." Then she gave her head a shake. "The guy you're describing would never make it through the academy."

"I have nothing left here. I've seen what I needed to see. You done?"

She nodded and followed me back to the living room. There I stopped and turned to her.

"There is one more observation. I think, if we can make the fine distinction between trusted and unthreatening, our guy is more likely to fall into the unthreatening category."

She frowned. "What makes you say that?"

"The fact that, as we said before, anyone who had become a trusted friend or acquaintance of all seven victims would have to have come to the attention of the investigating team. But this guy didn't. This guy is almost invisible. Mr. Cellophane. He is negative in every sense. Unnoticed and unthreatening. You'd open the door to him because you'd never believe he could hurt you."

"Yeah, we said that before, and I guess it makes sense, Stone. But I say again, this is a hell of a lot of assumption based on the way she might have opened the door." She raised a hand. "And I know I'm the one who raised the whole door thing. But still. It's all assumption."

I gave a small laugh. "You are absolutely correct, Dehan. But before we go, let me ask you something. If you lived here and Dave Clark rang at your door at ten at night, would you let him in?"

She studied my face a moment. "No," she said. "No woman in her right mind would."

I nodded, smiling. "How about if you'd met him at the store and got talking to him?"

"Even less. He is too weird."

"One girl, maybe, who goes for weird guys. But six? Out of the question. And then inspire a copycat?"

"No, no way."

I opened the door and followed her out. She said, "So what now?"

"We get Rookie Gordon to look into the religious beliefs and practices of our seven victims to see if they overlap at any point."

"I'm sure she'll do a sterling job," she said, making her way to the elevator.

"Meanwhile, you and I will go and catch up on our sleeping. We have been on our feet some sixteen hours, twelve of which we have been driving. I am done."

"Sounds good to me."

The doors clattered open, and we stepped into the grubby steel box again.

"However," I told her, "before sleep, I will require one of your exquisite moussakas and a bottle of oak-aged red wine."

She looked skeptical. "What's in it for me, big guy? Moussaka's a lotta woik."

"Woik?" I took the keys from her and climbed behind the wheel. She got in next to me.

"Yeah, if you' fwom the Bwonx in Noo Yoik, moussaka is a lotta woik."

"No arguing with that. Okay, you make me a moussaka and I—" I turned the key in the ignition and the big 3.8-liter beast growled. "I will mix you the best martini in Noo Yoik, and after dinner, I will massage your feet."

She grinned and gave a soft gurgle of a laugh, and we moved down the road toward the station house.

FIVE

Next morning, with Rookie Gordon set to work trawling through the religious persuasions of the Castle Hill Ripper's victims, Dehan and I took a drive to Shoprite which, though it claims to be at 1994 Bruckner Boulevard, is in fact on the corner of Story and Pugsley. We parked in the parking lot and hunched our way through the relentless drizzle and the sliding doors into the vast, sterile space inside. They'd been open since six, and at eight-thirty, they were busy already. Dehan showed her badge to a kid on checkout and told him, "We need to see the manager."

The kid nodded and smiled the way he'd been taught and grabbed a phone.

"Mr. Panayotes, there are a couple of detectives here to see you?" He said it like he was asking a question. He smiled at us while he listened to the answer. "Yes sir, detectives… I'll tell them that." He hung up and pointed into the store. "If you go to the last aisle on your right and walk right to the end, the manager's office is down there. But he is coming to meet you, along that aisle, so you should bump into each other before you get there."

I thanked him, and we made our way through enormous quantities of food and cleaning products down a long, shiny passage populated by zombies that were mainly gentle and harmless unless roused. About halfway there, we saw a large man moving toward us. He seemed to walk by throwing his knees forward while maintaining a dynamic of controlled instability. He wore a Shoprite shirt and an expression that said the world had made him mad, and the world was going to regret it.

"Are you the detectives?" he asked from far away in a strong Greek accent, long before it was reasonable to start talking. So we took another few steps before Dehan said, "Are you the manager of this store?" As she said it, we pulled our badges and showed them to him. "I am Detective Carmen Dehan of the New York City Police Department. This is my partner, Detective John Stone. We need to talk to you."

He clenched his forehead, like a fist, and his bottom lip stuck out. "Is it one of my staff? I'm not responsible for what they do in their private lives."

I said, "Mr. Panayotes. Can we go to your office and speak, please?"

He glanced at me resentfully, turned, and started throwing his knees back where he'd brought them from.

We pushed through a couple sets of doors of the type zombies swarm through in the kind of movies you don't want your kids to watch, and he led the way into an office you wouldn't aspire to. He waved a hand at a couple of chairs and sat behind his desk.

"Who is it and what have they done? First thing I tell them," he told Dehan, "don't cause me problems. Arrive on time, do your job, and don't cause me problems." He turned to me like the next thing he was going to say was something a guy would understand. "If I want you in my goddamn life, I'll marry you, right? Otherwise, when you step out of my shop, you step out of my goddamn life until tomorrow morning at five fifty-eight."

Dehan drew breath, but he talked over her. "AI is gone exterminate humanity? You know what I say? Good. *Good!*" He turned back to me. "Human beings are shit. *Skatá!*" He turned back to Dehan. "Excuse me." He turned back to me again. "Shit.

Human beings are shit." To Dehan. "Excuse me. All they do is make problems."

"You're not a human being?" I asked him, and he shrugged.

"I am Greek. Is different."

Dehan cut in, "Mr. Panayotes, we are investigating a series of murders that took place in this neighborhood between 2018, just after your store opened, and 2021."

"The Ripper, the Castle Hill Ripper." He shrugged. "You got the guy." He said it like we'd obviously not heard. "David Clark. He's in prison. I remember him. He work here. Stupid. You know what I say?" He leaned forward, staring first into my face and then into Dehan's. "Cut out his belly." He gestured with his open palm at his desk, like David Clark's belly was lying there. "See what he thinks then. Eh? With his belly cut out like the girls. This is what you like to do? Okay. So we do it to you. Still you like it? *Malákas!*"

"What we really need to know—"

"But the girls he kills? Pah! Whores! Each one of them is pregnant with a baby. I knew them. I knew all of them by name. They all come here, 'Hello, Mr. Pany! Hello, Mr. Pany!' Each one of them is not married. Each one of them is fuckin' around—" He shrugged and spread his hands to Dehan. "Sorry." Back to me, "Each one is fuckin' every guy in the Bronx for..." He rubbed his thumb against his index and middle finger in the time-honored universal gesture for money. "Eh? Eh? Fuckin' for money. What is that? Is a whore, right? If you are a whore fuckin' for money, sooner or later you gonna pay the price. They got what God send them, what they deserve."

I said, "Mr. Panayotes. We have some questions for you."

I held his eye till he shut up, shrugged, spread his hands, and made a face that pulled down the corners of his mouth. When he was done, I said, "During that period, 2018 to 2021, did you have an employee who was specifically employed for deliveries?"

"Yeah, of course." His hands were going again, gesturing out toward the shop. "I am not going to take staff from the shop, who are on checkout, filling shelves, workin' the bakery—"

"Mr. Panayotes." He paused. "Yes or no is fine. You had dedicated delivery guys."

"Yes."

Dehan said, "Now this is important, so I need you to think about it before you answer. Aside from delivering orders, did those guys have direct contact with the customers?"

He looked up at the ceiling, shrugged, and spread his hands. "Okay, I think about it."

"So?"

"No. I don't need to think about it, but you say think about it, so I think. The answer is the same like I don't think about it. No! I have three drivers. They come in. They get the orders, they fill the orders, they take them to the houses. Then they do again. Get orders, fill orders, take orders. No chattin', no makin' friends, no wastin' my fuckin' time."

"Okay, that's fine. Let me ask it this way, Mr. Panayotes. Between 2018, when the shop opened, and 2021, who was the most popular guy in the shop? The one all the customers liked, the one they all asked for help, the nicest, most popular member of staff with the customers? Who was that?"

He laughed again, a big, shouting laugh. He stopped, stared at me and then Dehan, and laughed again. "Easy! Same guy as now. Real nice guy, nothing is too much trouble, whatever you need he is there to help, twenty-four seven. He was here day one, he is still here today, and all the customers love him."

I glanced at Dehan. She said, "Can we talk to him?"

He grinned. "You talkin' to him already, darling. You're cops. You bringin' me problems. So I'm rude, and I have no time to waste on you. If you're a customer, you gonna buy something, nothing is too much trouble. What you want? Elephant sandwich? I'm gonna find elephant meat for you. What kinda bread you want? You want me to bring it to your house? No problem.

Nothing too much trouble. For customers." He smiled from Dehan to me. "You wanna buy something?"

"No. Do you ever do deliveries personally, Mr. Panayotes?"

"Nah." He flapped a hand at me. "I told you, I got three guys make the deliveries." He scowled. "What's the matter? You got Dave. Why you askin' questions now?"

Dehan said, "It's a routine follow-up. You never made deliveries personally, say on your way home from work, for a special customer?"

He narrowed his eyes. "Hey? What is this? You tryin' to put something on me? No, I never make personal deliveries. When I finish work, I go home to my wife. I'm nice to my customers, Mr. Pany, they call me, 'Hey, Mr. Pany, how you doin'?' but I don't make personal deliveries after work."

I nodded. "Okay, good. Now you have some idea what we are looking for, Mr. Panayotes, can you think of anybody during the 2018 to 2021 period who might have fit that bill? Popular, friendly, nothing too much trouble, might make a special, personal delivery after work…?"

This time, he thought about it. "No, these shit? No. Anyone like that is getting promoted, maybe runnin' a store somewhere. These fuckin' losers comin' in, workin' their shift then fuck off home."

"Dave, you said you remember him."

"Yeah. Is hard to forget Dave. Is too stupid to forget."

"Did he have much contact with the customers?"

"You kidding?" He stared at Dehan and laughed. "Is he crazy?" He turned back to me. "You outta your crazy mind? I ain't gonna—would you? I'm gonna let that freak near my customers? No, of course not? What am I—"

"Mr. Panayotes? Yes or no is fine. Did Dave ever do deliveries?"

"No."

I turned to Dehan and sighed. "Detective, could you give Mr.

Panayotes and me a moment? Go get me a coffee and a donut, would you? Wait for me at the car."

She puffed out her cheeks and blew. "Sugar?"

"No, I'm sweet enough."

I winked at the manager as Dehan left and, though his eyes were cautious, he laughed. I said, "Politics. Everybody knows they're no use, but we gotta have them as cops and in the armed forces, right? Politics."

"It's the modern world. Not just cops and soldiers! Now we got presidents, prime ministers, priests, bishops. An' let me ask you—where—right?—where are all the crazy fuckin' ideas coming from?"

I leaned forward, laughing, "Where they always came from! But before, they kept them in the damned kitchen. Now they're implementing them in the workplace, in local government, in *national* government, the courts! I tell you!" I shook my head. "You're lucky. You're the boss. I have to work with her. Hey!" I pointed at him. He jerked his chin in a kind of "What?" gesture. I said, "You know why women always marry in white?" He grinned and shrugged. I told him, "Domestic appliances always come in white!"

He laughed out loud, slapped his desk, and pointed at me. "That's good! I like that!"

I pointed at him again. "Woman is walking home at one p.m. Traffic light is green for her. She steps into the road and a car knocks her down. Whose fault is it?"

"It was green for her?" I nodded. "Driver's fault...?"

"No sir! It was *her* damn fault! That time of day she should've been home making lunch for her husband!"

That really had him roaring. I shared the laugh with him, and as it died down, I leaned forward, confidentially, two guys understanding each other, getting things done.

"Listen, you said earlier that the women Dave killed were whores. I want to ask you, is that something you know as a fact? I mean, you are in a privileged position here, this is a kind of *agora*, right? Like the ancient Greek market. And you are a very popular man in the community. So I imagine you hear things, see things, and I bet you're a smart guy. Not much passes you by, am I wrong?"

"Ah, my friend, you are not wrong. I don't miss much." He tapped the side of his nose with his finger. "I am observant man."

"So Sandra Gavilan, Tomasina Traubert, Nompumelelo Moyo…"

He was making a face like constipation. "Let me put it like this, they was not *professional* prostitutes, on the street corner, givin' their money to the pimps. Okay? They was *whores*. I am meanin' by this that if you got some money, nice car, if you gonna show them a good time, pay the rent, be nice and generous with them, they gonna go to bed with you. See what I mean? This is not a prostitute, but she is a whore. I have no respect for women like that."

"Yeah, I see, I understand. They were that kind of woman, huh?"

He hunched his shoulders, spread his big hands. "They're havin' babies. Where's the dad? Where's the family? What kind of a life you gonna give that baby? What kind of guidance, right? If it's a girl, what you gonna teach her? To be another whore like her mother? Nah, I have no respect for that."

I nodded. "I hear you." I handed him my card. "Listen, give me a call if anything comes to mind. And, don't take this the wrong way, it is pure routine. Can you tell me where you were on the night of April 30th to May 1st?"

"Sure. That was poker night. We meet, few friends, play poker. We was at Adonis's apartment."

"Adonis?"

He was scribbling on a pad. "Yeah, Tony. We call him Tony. Tony, Adonis, same thing." He handed me the piece of paper. It was a name, an address, and a telephone number. "You call him. He tell you."

I took it. "Thanks. You mind if I take a look around, talk to the workers?"

"You gotta do your job, right? We got nothing to hide. I was happy to cooperate with your other detective, Romano. I know him too. I'm happy to cooperate with you and your lady."

I stood and pointed my finger at him like a gun. "I'm grateful. Hang loose, Mr. Pany."

He pointed back. "Keep shootin' them bad guys, Detective Stone!"

I found Dehan sitting behind the wheel of the Jag drinking a black coffee. I got in the passenger seat and handed her the keys.

"Where is my coffee and donut, woman?"

"I ate your donut, and I am drinking your coffee."

"Nice." I looked through the windshield at the storefront in the rain. "I'm surprised Mike didn't focus in on Mr. Panayotes back in the day."

"This is going to sound like I'm being funny, Stone, but I am actually not. He probably recognized a kindred spirit. They probably got on like a house on fire."

I thought back to the performance I had just put on and said, "You could well be right."

She studied me for a moment. "You like him for it?"

"I would certainly have him high on my list of potentials. He seems to have an alibi for Sunday night. He was playing poker with Adonis."

"No kidding? I was having cocktails with Apollo and Aphrodite."

"Right. And he is very vocal about his contempt for what he calls whores, as distinct from prostitutes."

She handed me the coffee. "Let me guess. With a prostitute, it's a job; with a whore, she's a lazy bitch with no moral standards and deserves to die."

"Close enough. He certainly believes they got what they had coming to them. Whether these ugly thoughts are capable of swelling into homicidal passion, I wouldn't like to say. It's possible."

She pursed her lips and went abstracted, like she was seeing something in her mind. "It's not hard to imagine him delivering a leg of lamb after work, like you said, and taking payment in kind."

I sipped the coffee. "One of the last things he said to me was that they were all having babies. He said, 'Where's the dad? Where's the family?' And then asked what kind of a life they were going to give their babies. And if it was a girl, what were they going to teach her? He said, 'What they gonna teach her? To be another whore like them?'" I looked at her and winced. "Is that motive for murder?"

She gave her head a little twitch. "It's not the motive that counts, is it? It's the person who has it. For some people, it could be. He gets them pregnant, then kills them before they give birth." Then she added, "And in unconscious brotherhood, he and Mike frame Dave Clark." She looked away at the drizzle on the gray concrete. "That's dark."

"It is also more pure speculation," I told her, but there was a lack of conviction in my words. She had put her finger on it. It was not hard to imagine Sandra Gavilan peering through her peephole and seeing that big, smiling face holding up a leg of lamb, a couple of bags of groceries, whatever. She opens the door, he moves in talking, joking, "Now you're eating for two!" She closes the door and hurries over to make space on the coffee table...

It was not hard to imagine at all.

"C'mon," I said. "Let's go talk to the minions."

SIX

We didn't go back into the shop. We went around the back to the loading bays. There was a big truck docked there being unloaded, and in the second bay, a smaller truck was being loaded up with customer orders. I approached the driver while Dehan snooped around, largely unnoticed. He was maybe in his thirties, with dreadlocks and a beard that looked like it had started to grow, then changed its mind and decided to go back to bed. I showed him my badge.

"Detective John Stone, NYPD."

"Yeah?"

He didn't look. He kept loading his van. I said, "Can you spare a minute?"

He still didn't look at me. "What for? I got a lot of work."

"You remember Dave Clark?"

"Should I?"

"You going to give me a lot of attitude?" He dumped a bag in the back of the van and now turned to look at me. I told him, "Right now, I have zero interest in you, except I want to ask you two or three questions about where you work. Keep obstructing me, and I might acquire a deeper interest in you, which I haven't got right now. Have you got a problem talking to me?"

"No."

"Good, so take a break. If somebody complains, send them to me. Two minutes. How long have you worked here?"

"'Bout five years."

"Always driving?"

"Yeah."

"Okay, so I want you to think hard, 2018 to 2021. There's somebody working here who is really popular with the clients. Maybe he's a joker. Maybe he's just a nice guy who's into that whole 'Namaste' thing. Either way he's really helpful and kind, and everybody likes him." I raised one hand. "When I say everybody, I am talking about the customers. Maybe with the staff he is more withdrawn, but with the customers, he puts himself out."

Dehan strolled up and joined us and flashed her badge. "Detective Carmen Dehan, NYPD."

I went on. "Now, the important thing about this guy, and you, as a driver, might just know something about this, is that sometimes he might make private deliveries after work, on his way home, for example."

He hunched his shoulder and shook his head. "The only person who might be kind of like that is the manager, Mr. Panayotes. He's tough on the workers. I mean—" He looked away and shrugged again. "He can be a son of a bitch to the staff. But with the customers you'd swear he had a split personality. He's the nicest guy in the world." He gave his head a doubtful twitch. "But delivering things after work?" He shook his head. "I don't know nothing about that."

He closed up the van. "Only thing I ever heard about deliveries, like, unofficial deliveries, not us in the vans? Was when that chick across the freeway got stabbed Monday night."

Dehan crossed her arms. "What did you hear?"

"Somebody phoned to thank Mr. Panayotes for delivering some items a customer left behind. They was talking about it. You should talk to Oliver. He knows what happened." He pointed toward a couple of red fire doors in back. "He's in the staff room right now taking a break."

We thanked him and made our way across the loading area toward the two red doors. When we pushed in, several people turned to look at us. They were all wearing the Shoprite T-shirt. There was a big guy with a scraggly beard getting himself a cappuccino from a coffee machine. There were three women sitting together eating Chinese from Styrofoam containers, and there was a young guy sitting in an armchair reading a *National Geographic* magazine. We held up our badges. I said:

"New York Police Department, Detectives Stone and Dehan. Anybody here called Oliver?"

The kid in the armchair looked up and raised his hand. "I'm Oliver."

We approached and sat opposite him across a melamine coffee table. Dehan spoke.

"I am Detective Carmen Dehan, and this is Detective John Stone. We're working out of the 43rd precinct up the road."

"Sure. Is it about that poor girl who got killed Monday night?"

She hesitated half a second, then asked, "What do you know about that?"

"Just what I heard on the news. They're saying maybe you got the wrong guy two years ago, in the Ripper case."

I asked him, "How long have you worked here, Oliver?"

"Just a couple of years. We moved here from North Dakota in 2020."

Dehan gave a perfunctory nod. "We are interested in talking to people who have made unscheduled deliveries. You know, the guys in the vans are on the clock. They make the delivery during hours, right? They dump their stuff, and they're on their way. We're looking for people who might be a bit more involved in the community, meet people, talk to people, maybe deliver something as a favor after hours on the way home. Somebody who might have seen someone or something unusual. You know the sort of thing I'm talking about?"

"Sure. That doesn't happen, really. It would be viewed as bad policy. The only person who might have the discretion to do something like that would be Mr. Panayotes." He gave a small laugh. "I mean, I say that, but actually *I* did just that a couple of days ago, on Saturday evening. The very night before she was killed. I was close to the end of my shift. Elaine, that poor woman who was killed? She had come in earlier, in a rush, and when she took her stuff, she left behind a couple of items, some shampoo and a conditioner. Anyhow, we have her address on record, because she often has her stuff delivered, so I looked it up and, on my way home, I took the stuff and left it on her mat. She called Mr. Panayotes the next day, Sunday, to ask him to thank me. She was such a sweet woman. It says in the news that she was pregnant." He winced. "Awful. To think…"

Dehan was frowning. "So hang on a minute, Oliver. Are you telling me you delivered some items she had forgotten, to her door, the day before she was killed?"

"On my way home, yes."

"Have you ever done that before?"

"No, never. And though Mr. Panayotes congratulated me on Elaine calling up to thank me, he also told me I should never do it again. It is bad store policy, and I do see that now. Especially after what happened to her the very next day."

I scratched my chin. "Oliver, let me see if I understand this. Are you saying that, though you and the other staff don't make, as it were, unofficial home deliveries, maybe Mr. Panayotes does?"

He smiled and looked away at the wall. "Uh, no. I am not saying that. I have no idea at all whether any member of staff drops in on any of our customers after hours. But if anybody used shop business as an excuse to do so, the only person I could think of who would have the authority to do it would be the boss." He laughed and made a "what you gonna do" face. "Also, I mean, there's the *personality*, right? The rest of us? We just *work* here.

But Mr. Panayotes, he kind of *is* Shoprite Bruckner Avenue. He has this *huge* personality, and the shoppers just *love* him. He knows *everyone* by name. And I mean *everyone!* He's tough, but he is a superb manager."

I grunted, then, "You didn't talk to Elaine when you took her shampoo around?"

He shook his head. "No, sir! I didn't want to disturb her. Plus, Mom was waiting for me to get home. She doesn't like to be left alone. I left her purchases on the mat, rang the bell, and skedaddled."

Dehan had her chin in her hands and her eyes narrowed. "You live with your mom?" "For now, yeah. Like I said, we're from North Dakota, a little town in like the middle of nowhere called Drake. We moved here a couple of years back because I really want to further my education, go to college." He shrugged and gave an apologetic laugh. "Anyhow. So I work here to pay my way." He hesitated a moment, and there was sadness in his face. "Back home, dropping some groceries off to a customer on your way home is neighborly." He shrugged. "It's what you do. Here it's bad policy and perceived as threatening behavior. I guess things are different in the big city."

I nodded and smiled. "Things are different in the big city, Oliver. That is true. What time did she call? I'm surprised he didn't mention it."

"Elaine? Oh, golly!" He looked over at where the girls were sitting. "Sally, what time did Elaine Gallardo call to thank Mr. Panayotes...?"

"Uh, oh, you and me were on checkout, so I guess, half past ten in the morning? Eleven at the latest."

He turned to us. "We explained all this to the detective." He frowned. "Romano?"

"Yeah, Detective Romano." It was Dehan. She looked a question at me. I nodded and thanked him for his help. We went back out through the shop and into the drizzle.

Back in the car, I called Mike Romano.

"What do you want, Stone?"

"What's your estimated time of death for Elaine Gallardo?"

"Why?"

"Because I need to know. The chief—"

"The chief told me to assist you in any way I can on a review of the original *six* killings. Elaine Gallardo is *not* one of the original six killings. So my answer is, I don't remember, and, Stone, don't waste my time. I have a murder to investigate."

He hung up. "Son of a bitch."

I called Frank and put it on speaker.

"John, what can I do for you?"

"Good morning. What's the approximate time of death on the Gallardo girl? We were there at three in the morning."

"Yes, it's complicated. You know it's impossible to get time of death from the state of the body. Can't you ask Romano? He's the investigating officer."

"Yeah, I just asked him, and he told me to go to hell and stop wasting his time. Give me a break, Frank."

A quiet sigh. A rustle of papers. "Time of death is sometime between eleven a.m. that morning—"

"Sunday, April thirtieth."

"Correct. And three p.m. that afternoon."

"Between eleven and *three p.m.?* I don't understand. What about the smoke? Why were we alerted so late?"

"Triple-glazed windows, drapes, and heavy pile synthetic carpets. The smoke was contained for several hours before one of the neighbors coming home from a late shift saw it creeping under her door."

"So why three p.m.? How do we know that?"

"Because the egg timer was set to go off at three p.m. It went off, and she did not turn off the eggs. So she must have been dead. *Quod erat decidendum.*"

I frowned hard. "Frank, if that is your reasoning—"

"Not my reasoning. I am just the medical examiner. That is Mike Romano's reasoning."

"That is reasoning? If you put eggs on to boil, you put them on for between six and ten minutes, no longer. That being the case, she put the eggs on at fifteen minutes before three at the earliest. That means the guy arrived and killed her in the ten to fifteen minutes after she put the eggs on to boil."

"That sounds eminently reasonable to me, John. But the last time we know for a fact she was alive is eleven o'clock. And we know she was dead by three. So it's between eleven and three on Sunday April 30th."

I sighed. "Okay, thanks, Frank."

I hung up and stared at Dehan, who was squinting back at me. "The apartment was sitting there, full of that smoke, nearly *twelve hours?* And nobody noticed?"

I rubbed my face, shook my head, and fired up the car. "I bet that wouldn't happen in Drake, North Dakota."

"Yeah, I guess things really are different here."

"This is a mess. There's a place on Castle Hill, just over the bridge..."

"The Way."

"The Way. That's the one. Let's go get some coffee and talk about this."

Fifteen minutes later, I made an illegal U-turn at Chatterton Avenue and found a spot to park right outside the café. Dehan opened her door and climbed out, muttering, "Man! You're making illegal U-turns now? You must be in a bad way."

The drizzle switched to heavy rain as we ran the five strides across the sidewalk and pushed in, shaking water from our heads. Dehan grabbed a table by the window, under a map of the world, with her damp head just under Australia.

I said, "You want a double espresso and a bagel?"

"Yeah." She frowned. "No. You know what? I want a large cappuccino, and get me a salmon bagel. Tell him to put a slice of orange—hey, you got oranges?"

This last was directed at the guy behind the counter. He smiled and nodded. "Yeah, we got oranges."

"Give me a bagel with smoked salmon, a slice of orange, round"—she indicated with her hands what round was—"and"—she narrowed her eyes—"have you got Branston Pickle?"

"What now?"

"Branston Pickle, it's an English kind of relish…"

She trailed off. He was shaking his head. "Nope, I can do the orange, but not the Branston thing."

"Okay, that then, and mayo."

He paused. "Salmon, orange, and mayo?"

"Yeah."

He looked at me with slightly raised eyebrows. I said, "So one toasted bagel with butter, a double espresso, what she said, and a large cappuccino."

I sat. She was looking out the window. "I think it's the weather."

"Must be. You never drink cappuccino. Listen, we need to look into Panayotes' alibi. He says he was at a poker game Sunday night. But now it looks like she was killed much earlier in the day, between eleven and three."

She turned to face me. Outside, the rain hissed and raised a mist two feet off the road.

"Sunday morning, he was at work because he took the call from Elaine and went and told Oliver about it. Also the girl"—she clicked her fingers a couple of times—"Sally, she also saw him. They close midday on Sunday. So between ten-thirty or eleven on Sunday until his poker game, we don't know where he was or what he was doing."

The guy from the counter brought us our coffee and bagels. He gave Dehan a smile and a twitch of the head. "Enjoy."

"Yeah, thanks."

"I don't understand why Mike makes no mention of this guy in any of the reports on those six women. I'm going to call him again. If he keeps giving me trouble, I'll arrest the son of a bitch for obstructing a murder investigation."

"You'd do that."

"Not would, I will."

I picked up my cell and it rang. It was the chief. "Sir."

"John. There's been another murder. Hart Street, by Westchester Creek."

I put it on speaker. "So soon? That's just a matter of hours! Is Mike there? He won't want to see me, sir. I phoned him half an hour ago, and he told me to go to hell."

"I know. He called me. I've spoken to him. I told him if he doesn't cooperate, I'll hand the investigation over to you. I need this resolved, Stone. Get down there. Frank and Joe are on their way."

SEVEN

It was a straight run down Castle Hill to where it met Zarega at the YMCA and Castle Hill Park. We reached the creek without seeing any patrol cars, ambulances, or flashing lights. It was only when we took the corner at the end, where it turns into Hart Street, that we saw them. They weren't outside any house. They were where Hart Street turns into Howe Avenue, off the road among the trees, on the banks of the creek. I heard Dehan half-whisper, "What the hell…?"

There were two patrol cars, Joe's team's crime scene van, Frank's 1975 Ford station wagon, an ambulance, and Mike's RAM 1500. They had tape across the road and a tent set up by the creek.

I pulled up outside the tape and killed the engine. The uniform there recognized my car and raised a hand in greeting. Dehan had a look of mild despair on her face. She was pointing at Mike's RAM, raising her shoulders and giving her head small shakes.

"Why?" she said at last. "He lives in New York, for crying out loud. Why does he need a RAM, for God's sake?"

I smiled and went to open the door. "You know what his problem is, Stone?" she asked as I got out. She got out too and spoke to me across the roof. "He secretly wants to be Longmire. He has this fantasy that really he belongs in Wyoming, he's lean and dour and smart. When really he's a fat, stupid loudmouth who lives in New York."

The uniform lifted the tape for us, and we ducked under. We approached the tent across the mud and peered in. Mike was there and looked at me with no expression. There was a woman lying twisted on the ground, in a position you would not naturally fall into. There was not much blood, but she had a huge, L-shaped cut in her belly. Frank was hunched over her. Dehan reached in her pocket and pulled on some latex gloves.

I said,

"Dehan, you stay here and see what Frank has to say. Mike, can I have a word with you?" I pointed toward the shore. "Over there."

He sighed noisily. He pushed past Dehan and came out. "What is it, Stone? Maybe you can waste time on cases that are thirty years old, but the rest of us gotta work."

I gestured toward the creek and started walking. He followed me. When we were sufficiently far not to be heard, standing in mud and shingle, I turned to face him.

"You hang up on me again when I am conducting police business, you continue to obstruct my investigation, you continue to libel and slander me in front of my work colleagues, and I will personally arrest you and have you prosecuted; and I will sue you for every goddamn penny you own. I am giving you this warning as a professional courtesy. The next time you hear about this, it will be from my lawyers."

He drew a breath. I placed my index finger on his chest.

"Don't talk yet, bigmouth. You need to listen if you want to hold on to your job. I just got through talking to the chief, and I know he told you if you keep obstructing my investigation, he'll take you off the case and give it to me. I don't give a damn about that, but women are dying because of your stupidity and your incompetence. Mike, you haven't got my arrest record in your wet dreams. So you start cooperating with me now, or I will see to it that you are banned from law enforcement for the rest of your life. Is there anything about that which you don't understand?"

He made several attempts to speak, but fear, anger, and pride had all gotten logjammed in his throat.

"And here's one last thing, unofficial and strictly between you and me. The next time you mouth off at me in front of officers, I am going to beat seven bales of shit out of you. And *then* I'm going to sue you. Have we understood each other, Mike? Or do you want to make like a man and take a swing at me?"

I waited. He stared with rage in his eyes. I said, "Good, now come and explain something to me and Detective Dehan."

I got to the tent, and he was a few paces behind me. When I poked my head in, Dehan was hunkered down beside Frank. She glanced at me and stood. Mike came up behind me. Dehan said, "Obviously she wasn't killed here. Looks like the cause of death was the wound to the belly. She was pregnant."

Frank looked up. "She hasn't been here long. In this warm, damp weather she'd be crawling with parasites. *Prima facie* there don't seem to be any other significant wounds. I need to get her back to the lab, and I'll give you a report as soon as I can."

"Frank." He looked at me. Something in my voice made him pay attention. "It's the same guy. We still have a serial killer in the Bronx, and he is smart."

"Understood."

We stepped back out into the drizzle, and I jerked my head at Mike. "I'd like you to explain to me and to Detective Dehan why Mr. Panayotes, the manager of Shoprite, never even figured on your list of suspects. I have been through the six files, and I cannot find a single alibi for that man. As far as I can see, he was never even interviewed."

He shrugged. "Why would he be? He was never a suspect."

"That is what I am asking you, Mike. What was it about Mr. Panayotes that stopped him from becoming a suspect?"

He spread his hands like he was making a votive offering and looked up at the sky. "Give me strength. Am I crazy? I always thought you need a reason to *be* a suspect. Now you need a reason *not* to be a suspect!"

Dehan answered him, wiping drizzle from her eyes with her cuffs.

"How about the fact that he runs the shop that is at the center of the geographical area where the murders took place? How about the fact that he makes a point of being friendly and on good terms with all his customers? How about the fact that he knew, personally, each of the girls by name? How about the fact that they used to call him by a nickname, Mr. Pany? How about the fact that he considered them whores and believed they deserved to die? How about, Mike, the fact that according to the staff at Shoprite, the only person in the store who might make deliveries out of hours is the manager? Any *one* of these facts is a reason at least to interview him and get alibis."

"Hey, get off my case, will ya? I know the guy! I've known him for years. Hell, we do our shopping there. I've played poker with the guy. He's a stand-up citizen."

I snarled, "A stand-up citizen who happens to think that whores who get murdered get no more than what they deserve! Do you share those values, Mike?"

The blood drained from his face. "You just back the hell off, Stone. I caught the guy, and he confessed. This is a copycat, and you know it."

I leaned forward. "What I know is that you screwed up bad. Dave Clark is a fantasist. He can't tell reality from fantasy, and he has killed nobody. And if you had bothered to do some thinking with your brain instead of your dick, you would have realized that no woman, looking through her peephole at ten or eleven at night in the Bronx, was going to open the door to Dave Clark and let him into her apartment—much less if she had seen him at the shop, where he had *no* contact with the customers because he was so antisocial!"

He stared at me, glanced at Dehan and back at me again. "What are you going to do?"

"I don't know yet. But let's be damn clear about one thing, Mike: You will read me in and brief me on every damned detail of this case from now on."

A voice called from behind me. Dehan and I both turned. It was Joe approaching, holding a purse in a large evidence bag. He had several smaller bags in his other hand.

"What is this," he was laughing, "a detectives' convention? We have an ID. Who am I talking to?"

Mike started to say, "Any one of—"

I cut him short and said, "Me. Who is she?"

"You won't believe the name. Zeta Reticuli. Forty years old, resident at 1808 B Lacombe Avenue, just up the road. I am going to take all this to the lab to run tests. I shall email you scans and photographs."

Dehan said, "You got her Social Security number there?"

He held up a plastic bag with her card in it. She took a picture with her phone.

I turned back to Joe. "Any footprints?"

"We're looking. But"—he shrugged and gestured around him—"the rain, lots of people come this way. It's hard. We might get lucky."

He headed for the van, and I turned to Dehan. "Why the change in MO? Why move the body out here? Why so soon after the last one?"

I didn't wait for an answer. I pulled out my cell and called the chief.

"Stone!"

"The victim is one Zeta Reticuli, forty years old and pregnant. She was not killed here. She bled out somewhere else and was dumped here. Her residence is at 1808 B Lacombe Avenue. Sir, all the other victims have been killed at their homes. For some reason, he wanted to remove this body from the place where he killed her, which we should assume was her home. We need a warrant to enter and search the premises, now. Meantime, sir, while you take care of that, I believe we have probable cause, and I am going in. Please send backup."

He stammered a bit, and I hung up. I told Dehan, "Let's go." I told Mike, "Every detail. And we are not done."

We left him watching us as we climbed into the Jag and moved fast onto Howe Avenue. We covered the six hundred yards to Lacombe in less than thirty seconds and fishtailed onto the avenue with the horn blaring. I screeched to a halt diagonally across the road, and while I went and kicked in the iron gate, Dehan took the magnetic light from under her seat, stuck it to the roof, and switched it on. Then she pulled her piece and followed me down the path to the front door, which was set in the alley at the side of the house.

She squeezed past me and went to the backyard. From there, she jerked her head at me and said, "Kitchen door's closed. All the lights are off."

I examined the lock. It had not been tampered with. I took a couple of photographs with my cell. Then I pulled the Sig Sauer Dehan had made me buy and put a round through it. I pushed the door open and shouted, "*NYPD! Come on out!*"

The only thing I got back was the dull, dark echo of my own voice. I stepped through the door and switched on the light. I was in a small entrance hall. There were coats on a rack to my right and a straw mat on a green and white checkerboard floor. A stand with a tall mirror on my left. An umbrella stand with two umbrellas.

A door on my right stood closed. A door on my left opened onto a passage. At the end of the passage, I could see the kitchen with damp light filtering through a window over a sink. I moved down the corridor and opened the door to let Dehan in. She said, "What?"

"Nothing yet. I haven't checked the living room. No access upstairs yet."

She followed me back to the hall. She opened the door while I trained my gun on it. There was nothing, so I stepped through.

Then there was something.

It was a large room. On the right, there was a cold fireplace and a dead TV. At the far end, glass doors showed a wet lawn framed by tall pines. On the left, a flight of stairs led up to the upper stories. In the middle of the floor, there was a square carpet. On it were a sofa and a couple of armchairs set around a coffee table facing the fire and the TV. The coffee table was broken and it, the rug, the sofa, and the chairs were saturated in more blood than you'd think would fit in a person. There were no footprints to the stairs.

Far off, sirens began to wail.

"You want to make the call? We'll need Joe here. I'll check upstairs, but I'm figuring he's gone."

"He took her down to the river."

"And he didn't come back. Anything he needed to do, he did before he left."

She pulled her cell and made the call while she walked out to open the door. I went upstairs. There were three bedrooms and a bathroom. Two of the bedrooms were closed. The beds had bare mattresses covered in sheets of plastic, and the closets were empty. The third bedroom was all extravagant pink and white, with lots of bows and ribbons and more drapes than you would ever need on a window. The bed had been made, but somebody had sat or lain on it recently. There was nothing much to see, and I didn't want to compromise the scene for Joe. So I poked my nose in the bathroom, saw one toothbrush and lots of toiletries, and made my way downstairs again. No footprints, no sign of having changed clothes or showered.

Dehan was outside getting wet in the drizzle, talking on the phone. There were two patrol cars, and the officers were setting up the tape. I joined Dehan as she was hanging up.

"They're sending a team. Mike's on his way. What happened here, Stone?"

I shook my head. "I don't know. Let's go to the station. I want to see what Gordon's found about the religious lives of our victims. Then I want her looking up Zeta Reticuli's Social Security number." I made for the gate but paused and turned back to her. "But on the way, we stop at Shoprite. I want to know where Panayotes was this morning, and I want to know where he was Sunday after work."

As we were climbing into the Jag, Mike's RAM was approaching ahead of us. Behind it, I could see Joe's crime scene van. Dehan said, "Joe'll want to take the original crime scene. He'll have the second team down at the river."

I nodded and fired up the engine. Mike watched us drive past. We didn't wave.

I took it slow and steady up Soundview, letting my mind assemble all the pieces we had. By the time we arrived at Walgreens, my mind was telling me we had squat, and all the bits did not a picture make. I didn't turn right for Shoprite. I turned left for the station house. Dehan glanced at me. I didn't say anything, so she supplied the words.

"I'll call Shoprite and have Panayotes come in."

"Do that."

EIGHT

Gordon sat next to Dehan, opposite me, and took a deep breath.

"Sandra Gavilan, Angela Garcia, Maria Romero, *and* Elaine Gallardo were all practicing Catholics who all attended Holy Cross on Soundview and Randall. Tomasina Traubert was of no particular religion. I spoke to a couple of her friends, and they said sometimes she was an atheist and sometimes she was a Buddhist. Though she said Buddhism was more a philosophy than a religion."

She glanced at us both to see if we were going to agree or not, then continued.

"Nompumelelo Moyo, man, I had to work at pronouncing that. Nom-pu-me-le-lo Moyo, she was a member of the Church of Revelation on White Plains, and Caren Mitchell of Pugsley Avenue was neither religious nor spiritual. Her friends commented that the closest she got to religion was beer. Not an alcoholic, but working on it." She laid down her notes and made a small wince. "I can dig deeper, Detectives, if you want me to, but the impression I got, very strongly, was that as far as religion was concerned, there was nothing that connected all these women."

Dehan said, "That is sterling work, Gordon," with an absolutely straight face. "What we would like you to do now is to find out everything you can about this woman." She handed her the photograph of Zeta Reticuli's Social Security card. "Start with whatever you can get from her Social Security number, and then extend your search. Marriages, kids, boyfriends, everything you can get."

"Got it. Thanks, Detectives."

She took the photograph of the card and walked away, with her ponytail bouncing.

Dehan was on her phone.

"Dan? Hi, it's Carmen… Carmen Dehan." She rolled her eyes. "Yeah, I still have a bad attitude and all that shit. Listen to me. You still in vice…? Yeah? Good for you. The name Zeta Reticuli mean anything to you…? You're funny. No, seriously. You should do standup. Now stop wasting my goddamn time. I'm working. Aside from the planet crazies get abducted to, does the name mean anything to you?"

She rolled her eyes at me and sighed, then handed me the phone. "Sergeant Daniel Santos."

The voice was saying, "…maybe we could get abducted together, right? C'mon, Carmen, you know you always wanted—"

"Sergeant Santos?" The voice stopped dead. "This is Detective John Stone of homicide. I am Detective Dehan's partner, and, not that it has any relevance to her enquiry, I am also her husband. I am not going to pursue any inappropriate suggestions you may have made on this occasion, but I would ask you to send any material you have regarding Zeta Reticuli to my email. If this is inconvenient for you, I can always address the request to your superiors."

"No, Detective Stone, that will not be necessary."

"Good. On a personal note, Sergeant. You didn't know Detective Dehan had gotten married?"

There was a protracted silence.

"No, sir."

"Now you know. As I am sure you also know, there is a disciplinary board for sexually inappropriate behavior."

"Yes, sir."

"Personally, I am old school, and I prefer the old way of dealing with these situations. But nowadays, that kind of thing is frowned upon. In the old days, you got a bloody nose and a few fractured ribs. These days, you lose your job. Changing times, Sergeant. I hope we never have to have this conversation again."

I hung up. Dehan was watching me. Her face had a delicate trace of surprise overlaid with amusement.

"Your hormones okay, Stone?"

"Sure, why?"

"That's the second time in one morning you've come out beating your chest."

The internal phone rang, and she beat me to it.

"Dehan." She raised her eyebrows and gave me a nod. "Interrogation room three? Thanks, Maria." She hung up. "Panayotes the People Pleaser is here. Upstairs in three."

"Let's go have a chat. Maybe I can beat my chest at him."

We climbed the stairs and pushed into interrogation room three. Panayotes looked up, spread his hands wide, and hunched his shoulders.

"Wha's going on? I talk to you this morning. I tell you everything you want to know!" He watched us sit down still with his arms wide and his shoulders up by his ears. "Now you callin' me in, put me in this room...!"

"We asked you to come in, Mr. Panayotes, because we are rushed off our feet and we need your help. This room is where we interview everybody, suspects, victims, witnesses. Please don't be offended."

He made some noises and raised his shoulders a few more times.

"I didn't realize you and Mike were close friends," I said.

"Mike?" He smiled. "Mike Romano? Yeah, friends. Is not

like, *family*, but friends. Good guy. We play poker sometimes. I know him long time. From neighborhood, from the store."

"Sure. That's nice. Now the thing is, Mr. Panayotes, in his investigation of the Castle Hill Ripper, because Mike knew you, he knew you were one of the good guys, he didn't ask you questions he should have asked you." I gave a small laugh. "I mean, *we* understand that, the cops at the 43rd understand that, but the DA doesn't. And now, with this copycat murder down the road, the *skatá* is hitting the fan."

He gave a half-hearted smile and a shrug. "I don't understand. What questions?"

"Well, like, he should have asked you where you were on the night Sandra Gavilan was killed in 2018. And Tomasina Traubert that same year."

He pointed at himself. "Me?" He threw back his head and laughed out loud. "Me? You are serious?"

Dehan shared his laugh, which was more than I was able to do. "Not just you, Mr. Pany, you and everybody in Shoprite. Of course, it is much too late now, though if you could provide us with your whereabouts on those dates, it would sure be helpful. But above all, we need to know where you were Sunday morning and early afternoon, up to about three p.m."

His jaw sagged. "You, I, you, me... You are serious?"

I said, "We are very serious, Mr. Panayotes. Women are being murdered in our precinct. We cannot allow friendships with our detectives to hamper our investigations. Where were you on Sunday between eleven a.m. and three p.m.?"

"I was at home, with my wife. I leave the shop at eleven, ten past eleven."

Dehan said, "After you transmitted the message from Elaine to Oliver—"

He turned his gape on her. "Yes, she called. I go lookin' for Oliver. He is in the checkout. I tell him, is good customers are phonin' to say thank you to him. But he must not go to their houses."

"Right."

"Then I am get my case and my things and I am go home."

Dehan raised an eyebrow. "You didn't pass by Elaine's house on the way to receive her thanks in person?"

"No, no." He was shaking his head. "No, no, no." He said it a few more times, then, "I go home. Straight home."

"Is there anybody who can substantiate that?"

"Sub...?"

"Confirm."

"Confirm. I..."

I cleared my throat. "You said you went home to your wife."

"Well"—his head was on one side, and he gave a nervous laugh—"she is not here right now, gone to see her mother."

"Was she there on Sunday?"

"No."

I sighed loudly. "Neighbors? Did *anybody* see you arrive home?"

"Maybe. Maybe neighbors."

"What time did you arrive home? You left the store at eleven-ten or eleven-fifteen. What time did you get home?"

"Is"—he spread his hands like we were being unreasonable—"is Pelham Bay. two miles, maybe. Ten minutes, fifteen, twenty. Get in car, get out car, traffic, lights. I don't know. Half past eleven? Maybe eleven forty-five."

Dehan asked, "Where do you park your car? Out front? In the garage?"

"Like everyone. If I am gonna stay in, I put the car in the garage. If I'm gonna go out again, I leave it out front."

"You were going to play poker with friends. So you left it out front."

"Yeah."

I asked him, "Where was poker?"

"Tony got a nice house in St. Lawrence Avenue, near where the big interchange with the expressway, the railway, the Parkway. You know."

"I know." I nodded. "What time did you get there, Panayotes?"

"Nine, nine o'clock. More or less."

I leaned back in my chair. "So from eleven-thirty Sunday morning until nine o'clock Sunday night, you have nobody to confirm where you were."

He shrugged like we were crazy or stupid or both. "I was home."

"But nobody can confirm that, can they?"

He took his time, staring at us in turn, blinking, with the expression of a man who is realizing much too slowly that an express train is hurtling toward him. Finally, he said, "No."

"What about last night, Panayotes? Where were you last night?"

"What happen last night?" He looked from me to Dehan and back again.

"Where were you?"

"I was in my home."

Dehan arched an eyebrow. "With your wife?"

"No, she is still with her mother."

"Is there anybody, Panayotes, who can confirm that you were at home?"

"Okay. Okay! Okay!" He lifted both hands. "I am order pizza, I can show you on telephone." He pulled out his phone and scrolled through his calls. "Here, call to pizza takeout, eight-thirty." Dehan made a note. "Is deliver at nine. The boy is see me at the door. And ten o'clock I take out the trash and my neighbor is see me. We say hi."

I looked at Dehan. She shook her head. I said, "Okay, Mr. Panayotes. Thank you for talking to us. We'll be in touch if we need anything else."

"I can go?"

"Of course."

He nodded, stood, and left in a hurry, throwing his knees out in front of him. I went to the wall and stood staring at Dehan in her chair. She said, "You know, there is something pathetic about him. I kind of feel sorry for him."

I went up on my toes, looking down at my feet.

"Is it feasible—I am asking you as a woman, is it feasible that he makes a lot of women feel that way? Is his ghastly mix of childlike vulnerability and Mediterranean macho attractive to some women?"

There was horror in her eyes when she said, "If you're asking me do *I* find him attractive, dear God, no! If you're asking me might some women find him attractive, I suppose it's possible." We held each other's eye for a long moment. Then she said, "His alibis are about as watertight as fishnet stockings."

"I know. We are faced with two possibilities, Little Grasshopper. The Castle Hill Ripper has successfully evaded capture since 2018 because he happened to be friends with Mike Romano, and there was no skill or intelligence involved on his part. He has always been a lumbering fool, and he has never provided himself with alibis, but now, because we have removed Mike from the equation, he has been exposed as the sloppy careless dunce that he is."

"Is *all* that still possibility one?"

"Yes. Don't be impertinent. Or Panayotes is a slob whose wife has left him because she can't take him anymore, he happens to be friends with Mike Romano, and he has no alibis because he didn't kill those women."

She groaned and rubbed her face. "No other option, huh?"

"Not that I can see. We also have to ask ourselves, if Dave Clark was framed, and to me it sure looks like he was framed, was he framed by the Ripper or by Mike? If we go with Mike, are we saying that Mike's friendship with Panayotes is so great that he would risk his career by framing Clark and letting a serial killer go free?" I shook my head. "I don't like Mike, I think he's a lazy, sloppy cop, but I don't see him shielding a serial killer."

She was nodding. "But neither do we see Panayotes being

smart or resourceful enough to frame Dave Clark convincingly enough to get him convicted."

I sighed a heavy sigh. "I might be woefully wrong, Dehan. I have no clarity right now. If you asked me can I see Panayotes bribing his way into these girls' homes with bags full of groceries, I'd have to say yes, I can. Can I see him being screwed up enough to kill them when he gets them pregnant?" I shrugged. "I can't say I'd be amazed. He seems to have no regard for women he considers whores. So yeah. I can see him doing that."

She took over. "But can we see him as the Castle Hill Ripper? No. He just isn't smart enough or subtle enough."

"That's how I see it right now. But Dehan, I could be wrong. I could be way off target."

There was a tap at the door, and Gordon poked her head in.

"Detectives, I saw Mr. Panayotes leave. Am I interrupting?"

Dehan shook her head. "What is it, Gordon?"

"I had a look at Zeta Reticuli. She owned the house where she lived on Lacombe Avenue. She had been arrested several times over the years for prostitution. In 2008—"

I interrupted her. "Come in, Gordon. Sit down." I pointed at the table where Dehan was sitting, and she took Panayotes' chair.

"In 2008, she changed her name from Cristi Muñoz—with the squiggly Spanish n—to Zeta Reticuli and moved to California, where she apparently made a lot of money making adult movies. In 2013, she returned to New York and bought her house. After that, she would go to Cali once or twice a year to make a movie and then come back."

Dehan said, "That's good work."

"There's more. In December of 2021, she married one Xavier Pereira. The son of Portuguese immigrants. He has a record of violent crimes. Mainly fights, no armed robbery or murder, nothing like that. But he'd been in for a year at Attica and got out a month ago. Zeta divorced him while he was inside. He now lives on Barretto Street, Hunts Point. I was going to look into whether he had any contact with Dave Clark while he was inside, but I thought you'd like to know what I'd found so far. It seemed important."

I nodded. "That is extremely good work, Gordon. Type it up and put it on my desk, would you?"

"Sure!"

She jumped up and left with her ponytail bouncing more than before.

"Okay, Stone, what are the odds? What do you say Pereira will prove to be subtle and manipulative, or will he be a big hairy brute?"

"I guess we'd better go find out."

She stood, but I didn't move. She said, "What?"

"Why did he dump the body? He has this almost ritualistic methodology going. down to killing every six months and apparently taking a year off every two years. Everything is meticulously planned, foreseen, and executed: the plastic covers for his shoes, the showers, the notebooks filled with precise observations. And then, suddenly, he kills twice in as many days and dumps the second body by the creek. No footprints, no shower. What made him do that? Rage? Frustration?"

Or was it simply not him? I didn't say it, but I thought it.

"Let's go ask him."

NINE

Barretto Street runs from Barretto Cove on the East River, from the filth and grime of Jett Industries and the Environmental Protection Department on Ryawa Avenue, north to the Corpus Christie Monastery on Lafayette Avenue and the Hunts Point Recreation Center. Few see the irony inherent in this juxtaposition of names and their locations, though it was not lost on Dehan, who chortled noisily and waggled her eyebrows at me as we drove past.

"Hunts Point Recreation, huh, Stone? Huh?"

I didn't answer.

Xavier Pereira's house was about halfway down, at number 533, beside a large warehouse. The door was a steel grill over heavy glass at the top of five worn steps. Behind the glass, a heavy drape had been drawn closed.

I hammered on the door while Dehan peered through the windows, which also had bars and drapes. Nothing happened there, but next door, a guy in blue overalls appeared out of the warehouse, wiping his hands on a dirty cloth. He seemed like he might be amused but trying not to show it. "He's in," he said.

"Yeah?"

"He come in just after I started my shift at six this morning.

He ain't come out since." He jerked his head at an old white Golf GTI across the road. "That's his Rabbit. You cops?"

I showed him my badge. "Detective Stone. That's my partner, Detective Dehan. NYPD. Why?"

He shrugged, gazing across the road at the late morning sun on the redbrick warehouse wall across the way.

"Just curious. I know he come out of Attica just a few weeks back. Wondered if he was on his way back in again."

"You got any reason to suppose he might be?"

He grinned. "Besides two cops knocking on his door at eleven o'clock in the morning?" He shrugged. "Nothing you could take to court. But he has a bad attitude, and guys with that kind of bad attitude, it ain't long before they wind up in trouble."

I jerked my thumb at the house. "He been here long?"

"Few years. You probably know he's been inside for a year. Before that, he lived on and off with a broad in Castle Hill. They used to fight a lot, and when they fought, he'd come back here, get drunk, get into fights."

Dehan said, "Not your favorite neighbor, huh?"

"You could say that."

"Does he see a lot of women?"

He smiled and gave his head a twitch. "Uh, mainly on a professional basis."

"Right."

"You say he came in at six?"

"I was opening up. He pulled up in the VW and went inside."

"Alone?"

He nodded, then looked past my shoulder. "Listen, I gotta get back to work."

He slipped inside as a voice grated behind me, "Who the hell are you, wha's that sonofabitch been sayin'? Wha's he tellin' you?"

He was maybe six foot two. He was strong, with broad shoulders and powerful arms. His crew cut and his stubble merged into a kind of sandpaper effect all over his head and face. Red eyes peered at us, and the morning breeze carried an unpleasant mix of alcohol, tobacco, and stale sweat. Dehan looked at his bare feet and the sweat stains on his gray undershirt and muttered, "I guess it ain't subtle and manipulative." Louder she said, "Are you Xavier Pereira?"

"Who wants to know?" He leered at her and pointed at me. "You can come in. He waits outside."

She showed him her badge. "Detective Carmen Dehan, New York Police Department. This is my partner, Detective John Stone."

I showed him my badge.

He sagged. "Shit, man. I'm only out like a month, and already you gonna start on me?"

I said, "We need to come in and talk to you."

He turned and went inside, leaving the door open. I followed with Dehan just behind me. There was a powerful smell of cannabis, and when we went into the living room, through the gloom I saw a coffee table by the sofa with burnt aluminum foil, a grinder and papers. He waved his hand at it. "Personal use, right?" Then to himself, "Gimme a break."

There was a kitchenette at the end of the room. He went in, rubbing his hands over his scalp, and switched on an electric kettle. Dehan went behind the sofa, pulled back the drapes, and opened the windows.

I said, "Are you married to Zeta Reticuli?"

He looked down at the floor. "No." Then he raised his eyes to look at me. The change was palpable. "That bitch divorced me while I was inside."

"Have you seen her recently?"

He raised his eyebrows high. "You kidding me, man? What the fuck do I wanna see her for? She ain't got nothin' I want, and I ain't got nothin' for her." The kettle was spouting steam. It clicked, and he went and spooned instant coffee granules into a dirty mug, then added four spoons of sugar and hot water.

Dehan asked him, "Where were you last night?"

He grinned at her. "That's the only question you know? Where were you last night? I was somewhere you'd like to be, sweetheart. I was—"

"Stop." He looked at me. I went on, "That would be a mistake, Pereira. Where were you last night?"

He moved to the sofa and sat. "I was with my bitch."

"What's her name?"

"Sandy Shaw. That's funny, right? Like Sandy Beach."

"Where can we talk to her?"

"She got an apartment on Garrison and Faile." He gave us the address, and Dehan wrote it down. "I spent the night there. I'm straight now. I smoke weed for the pains, you know? I got pains from a hard life. But I'm lookin' for work, getting' my shit straight. You don't need to keep comin' around checkin' on me."

"You party last night, Xavier?" It was Dehan. He smiled at her. "Yeah, we partied. Give me your number, baby, and I'll call you next time. You can party right along with us."

"So you want to explain to me why you came home at six a.m.? What time did you leave the party, five-thirty? What kind of party was that? You said she was your bitch. You didn't stay the night?"

"Come on, man! Give me a break! The police tellin' me now what time I have to leave a party? I can't leave a party when I want to?"

I said, "Answer the question, Pereira."

He sighed loudly, and a waft of stale tobacco reached me. "Sandy was partying hard, man. She had a friend there, Black chick called Shevron or somethin'. They was goin' hard, music was loud, fuckin' reggaeton, and I was done, man. I just wanted to sleep. So I got in my car, and I come home. And that is, like, the end of the story."

"What time did you leave?"

"I dunno. When I got here, that asshole was opening up. So I guess I left at five-forty-five or five-fifty. How the fuck do I know, man? I wasn't lookin' at my damned watch."

I hunkered down in front of him and stared hard into his face.

"Did you know she was pregnant?"

There was absolutely no expression. His bloodshot eyes I could now see were a pale blue. They flicked over my face. After a long moment, he said, "Yeah, I knew. She told me while I was inside."

"Is that why you killed her? Because she was pregnant?"

"I didn't even know she was dead."

"When we go and talk to Sandy and Shevron, are they going to tell us you were there till nearly six? Or are they going to tell us they were partying so hard they don't know what time you left? Or maybe they're going to tell us you were so tired because you went out during the party and came back in the wee, small hours. What do you think, Pereira?"

"I think you're fishing and you don't got squat. Zeta was not a whore. She was an actress. I was bad to her, and I beat her. I get mad, and I go crazy. You shouldn't do that to a woman. When I went inside, she told me she wanted a divorce. I told her okay. She'd met some nice guy who didn't hurt her like I did. I understand that. Then she told me she was pregnant from that guy, and I wished her a lot of happiness for the future. That's it. I never seen her again, and last night I was partying with my bitch and her friend. Now unless you gonna arrest me with no evidence and based on your shit theories, I am gonna ask you to get the hell out of my house."

We rose and left.

SANDY SHAW's apartment was on Garrison Avenue, in an old, six-story apartment block with iron fire escapes, straight out of Gotham City. I found a spot to park outside the coffee shop next door, and we climbed the stairs to the third floor. There was an elevator, but it didn't work.

The bell beside the door didn't work either, so Dehan rapped with her knuckles. The next door along opened, and so did the one at the end of the landing. They only opened a few inches, then closed again. After the third rap, Sandy's door opened, also a few inches, and a very sleepy face in its late thirties that could have been pretty if it hadn't absorbed so much ugliness, peered out.

"What?"

We showed her our badges. "Detectives Stone and Dehan, New York Police Department. We need to talk to you and Shevron. Can we come in, please?"

She shook her head. "No."

She began to close the door again. I said, "This is a murder inquiry, Sandy. You don't want to look like you're shielding a murderer. And I know you don't want to be hauled in as a material witness. Let's keep this friendly. Ten minutes and we'll be on our way."

She sagged and sighed, swore colorfully, and slipped the chain from the door. Like Pereira, she turned and walked into the apartment, leaving the door open. Unlike him, she screamed at the top of her voice, "*Shevy! The cops are here!*"

She went into a comfortable living room and pulled open the drapes. There was a small dining table against the wall and a sofa facing a TV. In front of the sofa, there was a coffee table with the same kind of paraphernalia Pereira had had. Only here, there was also a mirror and a pewter box. She blocked our view of it, gathered it all up, and carried it out toward the bedroom, calling over her shoulder, "You want coffee?"

We didn't answer. A moment later, she came back. "Shevy's just getting up. You want coffee?"

I said, "We're good, thanks."

She pointed at a couple of chairs against the wall. "Pull up a pew. Siddown."

As she said it, she poked a cigarette in her mouth and lit it. She inhaled deep and held the smoke a second. I guess some habits are hard to break. A moment later, a Black girl in her twenties came out wrapped in a blanket. She squinted at us. Sandy moved over, and she sat down.

"What's the problem? Did we make too much noise last night?"

"I'm pretty sure you did, but that's not why we're here. Who was with you last night?"

They both went very still. After a moment, Sandy glanced at Shevron.

"There was us—"

Dehan said, "Nobody else?"

She hesitated. "Yeah, Xavi was here."

"Xavi? Xavi who?"

"Xavier, he's an old friend. We've been hanging out lately."

I asked, "Xavier Pereira?"

"Yeah."

"What time did he arrive?"

"Oh, uh..." She turned to Shevron, who said, "He was here when I arrived. Lunch. Twelve o'clock?" She looked at Dehan and said, "We had a tuna salad with garbanzo beans."

Dehan smiled with little feeling. "Yeah, that's what I was wondering, what you had for lunch."

"So then he left what time?" I asked. "He came and went a couple of times, right?"

Sandy shook her head. Shevron was chewing her bottom lip, looking out the window. Sandy said, "No, he was there right through. I mean, we went done some shopping, right?" Shevron nodded without meeting her eye. "We bought tuna, avocados, beans, nice bread—"

"Beer," Shevron added. "We bought beer too, and vodka."

"Then we come home, and he stayed right through."

Dehan asked, "What time did he leave?"

"Jesus, I dunno!" They both laughed and leaned against each other. "We were wild. It was like, almost dawn? He was wrecked, man. He was complaining the music was too loud."

Shevron said, "I heard Mr. Stevens get up to go to work. Xavi had gone just before that, right? So like five-forty-five, five-fifty."

I looked at Dehan, smiled, and shook my head. It wasn't a happy smile. I looked at Shevron.

"How old are you, Shevron?"

"Twenty-two."

"Do you know how long you could get for accomplice to murder?"

There was a long silence while they both stared at me. Eventually she said, "What?" All the blood had drained from Sandy's face. I gave a small shrug.

"He was stoned, right? When he left the first time. I don't know what time it was, but it was late, and he was stoned and drunk. So how careful do you think he was? He's not the most cold, calculating guy at the best of times, is he? So now he's been a year in jail, he's angry, frustrated, crazy, drunk, and stoned. His wife has not only divorced him while he was inside, she's pregnant with another guy's baby. So I am asking you, how careful do you think he was? If they find his blood, his hair, semen, fingerprints, anything that places him at her house during last night, you will both be charged as accomplices in providing and attempting to maintain a false alibi."

Sandy sat back with her hand over her mouth. After a moment, her eyes sought mine. "Zeta?"

"Yeah. Zeta. She was murdered last night at her home. You knew her?"

"We were friends. She managed to get out of the game, years back. She was an actress. She was doing good, making money." She raised her shoulders an eighth of an inch. "I mean, it was porn, but it was classy, you know? Good production values, and she never had to take clients she didn't like. She was doing okay."

"Did you know she was pregnant?"

"Yeah." Her face looked genuinely sad. "She was really happy. She—or he—was going to get a good private education. Best schools, college."

"Do you know who the father was?"

"She never told us." She turned to Shevron. "Did she?"

Shevron shook her head and started to cry quietly without making a show of it. Sandy put her arm around her. "She said we'd find out in due course. Those were her words, 'You'll find out in due course.' She spoke like that, kind of elegant. He was some kind of solid guy, pillar of the community type, with a good solid job and a nice house by the water."

Dehan said, "How did Xavier feel about that?"

She gave Shevron a squeeze. Shevron rested her head on her shoulder. There was no expression on Sandy's face when she spoke. "I don't know. We never discussed it."

Dehan laughed. It was short and not very pretty. "Are you kidding me? What, was Xavier studying Zen Buddhism at Attica? Because I gotta tell you, Sandy, I don't see any other way that guy is ever going to learn to control his feelings or keep his mouth shut. If he has Zeta's husband and her new baby on his mind, he is not going to keep his thoughts to himself."

Irritation contracted Sandy's face for a moment. "Well, if he talked about it, he talked to somebody else. He didn't talk to me. To me, he talked about parties and love and beer and grass. And that's it!"

I asked, "How many times did he leave and come back yesterday, last night?"

"None!"

I raised my voice. "Come on, Sandy! He's not worth it! He might have killed your friend, for crying out loud! *And* her unborn baby!"

She glared at me. Shevron curled into her and buried her face in her shoulder. Suddenly her weeping was getting noisy.

"He arrived noon. He left at five-fifty. If he went out in between, I was too stoned to notice. You've asked your goddamn questions. Now get out!"

I sighed, and we stood. "It's fifteen to twenty, Sandy, for you and Shevron." I tossed her my card. "Think about it. Give me a call if you change your mind."

"I asked you to leave."

TEN

Dehan had the door of the Jag open, and I had the driver's door open. The rain had stopped, but the gray air was spitting, and I could see droplets accumulating on her hair. She wiped water from her right eye and said, "Are you going to get in, or are you just going to stand and look at it?"

I frowned at her.

"Yeah." I got in and slammed the door. She got in beside me, and as I fired up the Jag, I said, "Call Mike."

She put it on speaker, and I heard it ring three times. Then, "Mike Romano, who is this?"

"Mike, this is Stone. Zeta was seeing some guy, pillar of the community, nice car, steady job. Apparently, he got her pregnant. Talk to the neighbors, see if they can—"

"We bin talking to the neighbors already. It's what we call standard procedure. I did make detective, you know, Stone."

"Save it. I'm not interested. What did the neighbors say? Did she have a regular visitor?"

"No. Her visitors were few, and they were women. She used to go out regular in her car, but she had few—"

"Is Joe still there?"

"Yeah, he's right here. We were just—"

"Hand me over, would you?"

There was some muttering. I heard my name mentioned, then, "Hey John, what can I do for you?"

"You're still at Zeta's, right?"

"Yeah, but I'm on my way back to the lab. We're about done here."

"She has a garage at the back of the house, am I correct?"

"Yes, sir."

"Have you looked inside it yet?"

"The boys are on it now."

"There's a car."

"A Mercedes C-Class, about five years old."

"It has GPS."

"Yes."

"I need a printout of all the places she used the GPS for over the last year."

"Okay..."

"It's urgent. It's very urgent."

"I'm on it."

Dehan hung up and said, "However much lace she wears, she's a whore in the eyes of neighbors." I nodded. She went on. "So he doesn't want to be seen going to her house. Instead, she goes to his house."

She was narrowing her eyes, questioning what she was saying as she said it. After a moment, she said, "That's kind of backward, Stone, isn't it?"

"What do you mean?"

"Well, usually, as far as I am aware, men who see prostitutes see them in motels, or at the prostitute's apartment, because they don't want the *prostitute* to be seen at *their* house. But this guy is doing it backward." She stared at me while I drove, then added, "*He* doesn't want to be seen at *her* place. But he doesn't mind *her* being seen at *his* place?"

"Yeah, that is kind of backward." I glanced at her. "If that were so, what would it mean?"

She thought about it. "Well, the first thing that comes to my mind is that she is not known where he lives."

I nodded. "That makes sense. Anything else?"

After a moment, she turned to look at me. Her eyes flitted over my face. "Yeah, he *is* known where she lives, around Castle Hill."

She frowned hard at the passing shop fronts, at the people with hunched shoulders and collars turned up against the drizzle. The wipers scraped across the windshield and thudded back. I smiled.

"You're thinking now, how does this tie in with Elaine and the other six girls?"

"Yeah. You got some idea? Because I gotta tell you, Stone, right now, my head is spinning. This guy has suddenly turned his own MO on its head. He is a pillar of the community and he is *dating* his victim?" She shifted in her seat and turned so she could squint hard at me.

"Let me get this straight in my head. Don't talk. Just sit there and smirk and look self-satisfied. This guy, we'll call him Bob, decides in 2018 that he is going to start killing pregnant women. The Bureau has no comparable MOs anywhere in the country before that."

I nodded and tried to smirk in a self-satisfied way but said nothing.

"So he kills twice, and very successfully remains undetected. He takes a break during 2019. Maybe he thinks he got it out of his system. Whatever, he takes a break, but 2020 he's back, and over the next two years he kills four girls. All within an area of, what, a square mile?"

"Half a square mile."

"Right. What connects all the victims is where they buy their groceries, at Shoprite. We are even thinking that maybe he brings them stuff from the shop and that's how he gets in. Tell me if I am going wrong somewhere."

"You're dead on track."

"So he is in there, among these women, making contact with them but invisible."

"Right."

"And now, suddenly, he is a pillar of the community—that is hardly invisible—and he is *dating* his victim? But he doesn't want to be seen with her in the neighborhood. Does that make a lot of sense, or no sense at all? I mean, Stone, maybe, *maybe*, that is what he has been doing all along?"

She paused. I was thinking, not looking particularly self-satisfied. She said,

"I can't be seen going to your place. It would affect my job. But you come to my place. When I've squared it with my bosses we can get married, whatever. And the girls are so desperate to get out of the squalor they are living in, they buy anything he tells them."

"You've done everything but name him."

"Right?"

"Where does that leave Pereira?"

"Exactly where he said he was, getting out of his head with the Fokkens twins. And before you start lecturing me about being inappropriate, they are real twins, in Amsterdam. Louise and Martine Fokkens. F-O-K-K-"

"Yeah, that's fine, Dehan. Let's stay on track."

"I'm on track. E-N-S. Pereira was doing exactly what he and the girls said he was doing. Meanwhile, the baby's father was taking care of business."

We pulled into Fteley Avenue and parked. I regarded Dehan because she was the nicest thing to look at while I was thinking.

"Let's see what her GPS says."

When we got to our desks, Gordon's report was waiting there for us, two copies, one each, and as we lowered ourselves into our chairs, Gordon and her ponytail appeared at a brisk walk.

"Detectives, I thought I had better mention something. I typed up the finding I mentioned to you upstairs, but while I was at it, I thought I might as well call Attica and ask if Pereira was known to associate with any other prisoner. I thought it might not be significant, but on the other hand, if he associated with Dave Clark, then that might be very significant."

Dehan said, "That's very good work, Gordon" without a trace of irony. "What did they tell you?"

"Thank you, Detective. It was a matter of record because Clark does not associate with anybody, and his behavior is observed and noted by his therapist. He and Pereira did have contact and were known to talk to each other."

"Son of a gun!"

"They put me through to the psychiatrist, a Dr. Feldmann, and I asked him to email you the relevant part of the report. He was reluctant, but I pointed out it was relevant to a murder inquiry." She pointed at the printed pages. "It's all there in the annex."

"Keep it up, Gordon," I told her. "That's the way it's done."

She smiled. "This is an interesting case. If you need anything, please keep me in mind."

Dehan raised a hand. "Gordon, you can check this out. Call..." —she leafed through a notebook—"Pizza Take Out, East Tremont Avenue. Talk to them, see if a Mr. Panayotes with this number called last night about eight-thirty to have a pizza delivered."

"Sure thing, Detective!"

I watched her ponytail bounce out of view among the uniforms and turned to Dehan. "You were saying about Pereira doing what?"

Before she could complain about my self-satisfied smile, my cell rang, and I picked it up.

"John, it's Joe, from the lab."

I put it on speaker and set it on the desk between us.

"You get anything from the GPS?"

"Well, that depends what you were hoping for. She didn't use the GPS. The mileage on the car is minimal. I think she used it to go shopping once a week, and that's about it. The only major trips are two trips to Los Angeles, a place called Bellamour Ranch, Angelo Drive in Beverly Glen. And then, about a year ago, she drove to—are you ready for this? Poopy Bear's house, Quincy Avenue. I've emailed you the printout, but that's it. Those are the two addresses she used the GPS for."

"Thanks Joe, that's really helpful. You'll send me the full report when you're done."

"Will do."

I hung up and sat looking at Dehan, who sat looking back at me. After a moment, she said, "Poopy Bear."

I held up two fingers.

"One, we wake Pereira from his post-Fokkens slumber, we bring him in."

"Okay."

"We also pull in Sandy and Shevron as material witnesses. We let them see each other and then we interrogate them simultaneously, leading each to believe the other two are selling them out. And for good measure, we tell them Dave Clark has decided to talk."

She nodded. "Sounds good to me."

"If we play it right, it might pay off. Two, we take a drive over to Quincy Avenue. I think the guy has a right to know what happened to his girlfriend."

"Yeah." Her face went like stone. "And his unborn child."

I picked up the phone and called the chief.

"John."

"Sir, I want to bring Xavier Pereira in—"

"Who?"

"Zeta Reticuli was murdered last night."

"Yes, I am aware."

"Xavier Pereira was her ex-husband. He spent the last year in Attica, and it seems he struck up a friendship with Dave Clark. While he was inside, his wife divorced him and became pregnant from another man."

"That is very suggestive, John. Good work. What do you plan to do?"

"He has an alibi. He says he spent all day and all night with a couple of…professional ladies."

"You mean prostitutes."

"That's what I mean. They back up his story. What I want to do is pull them in as material witnesses and pull him in too, split them up, and work on all three at the same time, playing them against each other."

He was quiet for a bit, then, "Have you any concrete grounds for believing they are lying?"

"Yeah." I was thinking on my feet and said the first thing that came into my head. "The party amounted to twenty-four hours of vodka, beer, marijuana, and coke. At the end of twenty-four hours, the girls claim they were still going strong, and he left in his car because he didn't like the music they were playing. I believe that is physically impossible. It's impossible one bottle of vodka lasted them twenty-four hours, and it's impossible that after twenty-four hours of that kind of party, they would still be dancing and he would be capable of driving."

He grunted. I went on.

"Also, when he arrived, his car came from the wrong direction. It came from the south instead of from the north, which it would have if he was coming from her apartment."

He was silent again. "Barretto Street? He would come from the north if he was coming from Zeta's house too, over the railway onto Leggett and Randall."

"Unless he took the truck route and came down Hunts Point Avenue."

"And missed Randall because he was so upset? You're reaching, John."

"I'm thinking on my feet, sir. We need to get those three in separate interrogation rooms. I know Shevron will break under pressure."

"Shevron..." I heard him sigh through his nose. "Where do they get their names? All right, John, but this is still Mike's case. This is precisely what I did *not* want to happen. I'll tell him to bring them in as material witnesses. This had better pay off. *We are sailing by the seat of your pants!*"

"Yes sir. He can take a couple of cars to pick up Sandy Shaw and Shevron. Dehan and I will go get Pereira."

"All right, John. Keep me posted."

I hung up, and Gordon showed up at a run.

"Sir, Detective—"

"Yes, Gordon."

"The pizza takeout confirmed the order. Um, I heard you're sending out some cars to pull in some possible witnesses on the Ripper case?"

"Possible witnesses, yes."

"Can I go sir, please? I need the experience. I will not get in the way. I will make myself useful. Please!"

"Don't call me sir. Hang on." I looked at Dehan, who was talking to one of the patrol teams who were to accompany Mike. She nodded and turned to the big blonde. "Hey, Gunther, Gordon wants to ride with you. She needs the experience, and she's useful. Take her along, will you?"

He smiled at Gordon. "Sure. Just do exactly what you're told. And if anything goes down, keep low. Get your shit together. We're boarding at gate three."

Gordon ran, and Dehan asked me, "Are you armed?" I nodded. As she shrugged on her jacket, she added, "Pereira is a not a guy you want to take chances with."

"I know, Mom."

She didn't laugh. "I want to do something, Stone."

"Yeah?"

"We bring Pereira in. We tell him what's going down. Then we go to Quincy Avenue. We let Pereira sweat, and we have a look at this guy Zeta was with."

"Sure. I agree."

We made our way out to the car, and as we pulled out and headed for the expressway, I asked her, "Any special reason?"

She screwed up her face. "Yeah, but I don't know what. Something about it is getting on my nerves. Out there, in Pelham..." she said, and trailed off and shook her head. I didn't say anything, but it was needling me too.

There wasn't much traffic, and it wasn't long before we were pulling up outside Pereira's house again. We hammered on the door and on the windows, but all we got was an empty echo inside.

"The Golf isn't here." It was Dehan pulling her cell from her pocket. "I'm going to issue a BOLO. You want to talk to your friend in the warehouse?"

She walked away toward the Jag with the phone to her ear. The same guy in the blue overalls was coming out, wiping his hands on the same rag. He watched me approach and grinned.

"You left something behind, Detective?"

"Yeah. You seen it?"

"He went out ten minutes after you left this morning. Got in his car and headed out burning rubber. He hasn't been back since. You want me to give you a call if he shows up?"

I fished out a card and gave it to him. "Thanks, but don't take any risks. This guy is dangerous."

"I know he is. I'll let you know when he shows up."

"Thanks."

I went back outside. Dehan was approaching, shoving her phone in her pocket. "Anything?"

"He went out just after we left. Seems he was in a hurry. The guy here's going to give us a call when he shows up."

"*If* he shows up. He could be on his way to New Mexico for all we know." I thought about it a moment, chewing my lip. As I drew breath to speak, Dehan said, "We go back and talk to the girls when they bring them in, but meantime, we pass by Pelham Bay and look in on Quincy."

I sighed. "Yeah, okay, that's good."

I said it, but it felt wrong. Everything felt wrong. I didn't know why, it made no sense, but it was a feeling I couldn't shake.

ELEVEN

We took Bruckner Boulevard, crossed the creek, and took a right into Quincy. All the way, I had a growing sense of unease. We moved down at a steady pace, through what looked like a slice of New England transposed to New York, higgledy-piggledy houses, redbrick and clapboard, with their gabled roofs, wind vanes, and well-kept lawns.

It was as we came to the intersection with Barkley Avenue that it dawned on me, and it must have dawned on Dehan too because I heard her swear softly.

"Sweet Jesus, Stone. How could we be so stupid?"

"Pelham Bay, Quincy Avenue."

"I was looking at the damned address when I gave it to Gordon. It just didn't register."

We crossed Barkley, moved fifty yards down Quincy, did a one-eighty, and parked facing the house. Dehan was shaking her head.

"Listen to me. Don't interrupt, okay?"

"Okay."

"I said don't. Listen. Zeta is living in Castle Hill, making a couple of films a year in Los Angeles and cleaning up financially. She likes a bit of the rough, so she hooks up with Xavier Pereira.

That's a couple of years back. Like he told us, they have a complex relationship. Sometimes he stays at her place, sometimes he has to get out and go home. So when he's not around, she goes shopping at Shoprite and gets friendly with Mr. Pany and develops a taste for stuffed vine leaves. When Pereira gets put away for a year, they progress from dolmades to kleftiko, and things start to get serious."

I nodded. "She's got a lot to offer Mr. Pany. Aside from a wealth of experience in areas of life which he would appreciate fully, there is also her financial wealth, which he would not find unattractive either."

"But," she went on, "he is well known in the neighborhood, at least he thinks he is, and he cannot be seen to be consorting with a lady of the night, otherwise known to him as a *whore!* He is also not keen for Pereira to discover who has been cuckolding him while he has been in the slammer. So he and Zeta agree, provisionally at least, that they will meet only at his house, and he will not be seen at hers. She divorces Pereira and tells him she is pregnant with another man's baby."

"Right," I said, "and the sixty-four-thousand-dollar question is not so much what happened when she told Pereira, but what happened when she told Mr. Pany?"

She nodded slowly with pursed lips. "Was she a hard-working actress to him, or was she a whore who deserved to die?" She turned and stared at the house. "He would have had plenty of time to order the pizza, go and kill her, and get back home."

"Dumping the body would not be easy."

She looked at me. "The garage at her house is in back. He drags the body out and dumps it in the trunk. Nobody would see him. He takes it home, showers, dumps the clothes, then in the small hours, he takes her body and dumps it at the creek."

"And he does this because...?"

"Because he has a psychotic loathing of what he considers pregnant whores."

I thought about it, turning it over in my head. "No," I said.

"Why does he dump the body? Why doesn't he leave it where it is, put plastic bags on his feet, and go shower? Why does he dispose of the body? It's a stupid thing to do."

"Because…" She trailed off.

"I mean, are we saying that Panayotes, the manager of Shoprite, is the real, actual Castle Hill Ripper…?"

"Stone, he was in a perfect position to frame Dave Clark. He knew him, he knew how susceptible he was, and let's face it, Panayotes has a very powerful personality. He could easily make Dave sing and dance to his tune. And we've been told already that the only person in a position to make afterhours deliveries was him, and *he* has told us himself that he knew all the victims personally, and they all called him Mr. Pany."

I drew breath, but she cut across me. "That leaves the question we've been asking, which you've just asked me—why the change of MO with Zeta? Why the different behavior? Well, now we know why—"

"We do?"

"Yeah, because he started a serious relationship with her, and she got pregnant." She pointed at me. "Two gets you twenty, Stone. To that guy, on some weird fucked-up level in his unconscious, getting pregnant is a betrayal."

"That's deep, Dehan."

"*I'm* deep, Stone."

I leaned back, closed my eyes, and stared into the top of my skull.

"So if you are right, Pereira's alibi is going to prove to be true."

"Not necessarily. He could have fabricated it because he knew he was the obvious prime suspect."

I shook a finger, still with my eyes closed. "He already had the alibi set up *before* we arrived. The girls knew what to say."

"Okay, so he was doing something else, selling dope, whatever."

I grunted. "Okay, let's go talk to the Fokkens Twins, then

we'll come back and talk to Mr. Dolmades Kleftiko about his ex-girlfriend."

I fired up the Jaguar, and as I did so, my phone rang. The screen told me it was Mike. I put it on speaker and pulled away.

"What is it, Mike? I haven't got time for a turf war."

"That can wait. We have a situation. Fail Street, 847, Shevron's place. I don't know what the fuck you stirred up, Stone, but you'd better get here and sort it out."

"We're on our way. What's going on?"

"Just get here."

He hung up. Dehan grabbed the siren from under her seat and stuck it on the roof, and we did better than a hundred along the expressway before peeling off onto the Boulevard and exiting onto 163rd, where I fishtailed nicely into Hunts Point Avenue, accelerated hard and fishtailed into Seneca, accelerated again and fishtailed into Faile Street, and started to brake. Because a hundred and fifty feet in front of me, there was a police barrier with a SWAT van, four patrol cars, a lot of uniforms with body armor—and Mike's RAM.

I stopped sixty feet from the action with my hazard lights on and told Dehan, "The body armor in the trunk. Get a vest on, will you? And get mine for me."

She went to the trunk, and I climbed out. Mike was approaching. I said, "What's going on?"

He jerked his head at a big, dilapidated redbrick building. The doors and windows had been boarded up and then broken through to create a squat. It made you depressed just to look at it. Living in it was something I couldn't imagine.

"Your pal Xavier Pereira is in there."

"With Shevron?"

"Yeah, with your friend Shevron and her girl Sandy. He has a gun. We seen that. He says he has other weapons, if we go in he'll start shooting, and if we get inside, he kills the girls. You satisfied?"

I narrowed my eyes at him. "I don't understand your question. You want to explain that for me?"

He pointed savagely at the building. "You brought this on, Stone. You can't leave well enough alone! You have to keep—"

He stopped dead because I was waving Dehan over, and I had my cell in my hand, putting it to record.

"Dehan, come here, Mike is just explaining something to me. He wants to explain to me how I made this happen. He wants to explain how my not leaving well enough alone brought this on... You want to continue, Mike, now that we have a recording device and a witness?" He made an ugly face and flapped a hand at us. I pressed him, "Then, if you're done, would you please brief me on what has happened here?"

His neck and his cheeks were flushed. He stared at the cell in my hand and at Dehan standing beside me. He knew that every second of recorded silence was a stroke against him. He cleared his throat and said, "You wanna turn that damn thing off?"

I turned it off and put it in my pocket, then I went and stood real close to him, looking in his eyes. "Speaking of friends, Romano, remind me to fill you in on your pal Panayotes' relationship with Zeta. Now, brief me, please."

Dehan handed me my body armor and helped me put it on. We approached the cars that encircled the entrance to the building. There were maybe half a dozen cops hunkered down there with their pistols drawn and another six SWAT men gearing up behind their van.

Mike pointed at the door of the building. "She's got two rooms and a john at the back of the building, on the left."

"Through that door, at the back on the left?"

"Yeah, that's what I said. The car got to Sandy's place on Garrison. There was nobody there. It's like three hundred yards up the road. Meanwhile, we are here and we go and knock on Shevron's door. There's a shot. A slug goes right through the door and hits the ceiling. Pereira is in there, telling us to get the hell outta there or he is gonna start killing people. So we came out, I told the guys who went for Sandy to join us, and"—he gave me a look like he wanted to rip off my head and spit down my throat—"I hope you don't mind, Stone, I called SWAT before I called you. No offense, right?"

"Stick to the facts, would you, Mike? Do we know if there is anybody in there besides Sandy, Shevron, and Pereira?"

"How would I know that? I just got through telling you we didn't get inside."

Suddenly my belly was hot, and I was fighting to keep control. I leaned in close to him and whispered, "Mike, when this case is over, we can go out to Tallman Park, and you can try to beat me to death with your bare hands. Until then, keep your damned attitude to yourself and answer the damned questions. I don't know how you would know. That's why I am asking. Now stop wasting my time, or I swear I will have you taken off this case."

He leaned close. "You got yourself a date, Stone." He pulled back. "As far as we know, it's just the three of them in there."

"What about the adjoining rooms and apartments?"

"They've been cleared. The building is empty. I say we storm it."

"I want him alive."

His face flushed almost purple. "Stone, goddammit! This is still my—"

I walked away from him to the SWAT team and found the commander. "Captain, the man in there holding the hostages, I need him alive. So we hold fire until the chief at the 43rd tells us how this goes down. We clear on that?"

He frowned at me. "Who's in charge here?"

"Sir"—I was speaking into my cell—"I need you to take charge of the situation we have at Faile Street. Somebody is going to get killed, and I think it might be our three most valuable witnesses."

He sighed loudly. "All right, I'm on my way."

I hung up and turned to the SWAT commander. "The superintendent is on his way. We don't kill anybody here until he says so."

I turned to Mike. "What communication do we have with Pereira?"

He was shaking his head, drawing a breath. I turned away from him and called Joe. It rang three times.

"John, what can I do for you?"

"Urgent. Very urgent, Joe. In Zeta's possessions, there must be a telephone number for her ex-husband, Xavier Pereira."

"I'll check her phone."

"Make it snappy. We have a hostage situation, and I need to talk to him fast."

I went and found Dehan. She was hunkered behind a car talking to Gordon. As I approached, my phone rang. The screen didn't tell me anything. I answered, "Yeah, Stone."

"I'm gonna kill 'em. I'm gonna kill 'em both." Suddenly he was screaming. "*I'm gonna cut out their fuckin' bellies! Are you hearing me?*"

"I'm hearing you, Xavier. What do you want? What do I have to do to stop you from doing that?"

I was waving to Mike and the captain while I spoke. I put the phone on speaker and hunkered down beside Dehan and Gordon.

"What do you need to...? What? You gonna play psychological games with me now? You think you can play me? You think you can patronize me, and play me, and talk to me all calm and take me off my *fuckin' guard?* And creep up behind me, sweet and quiet, *and stab me in my back! Again and again until I am dead!*"

Mike and the SWAT commander had come up and gotten down beside me. I was saying, "Xavier, make no mistake. I am not humoring you or patronizing you. I am scared, because I have seen, and know very well, what you are capable of. So I am very scared. And you and I know, we both know, that what we see on TV, what they tell us goes on, has nothing to do with what really goes on."

"What...w-w...what the fuck...?"

He was confused, struggling. I said, "What I am trying to communicate to you, Xavier, is that we both know that whatever they say on TV, they *will* negotiate if they need to, to save their political careers. So what I am telling you, Xavier, is tell me what I need to do to save Sandy and Shevron. Am I getting through?"

Silence. I went on.

"And listen, man, I tried real hard, but I could not break them. They stuck by you, man. You partied solid and never left, even when I threatened them with accessory to murder. They lied for you, man, risked a long stretch for you. You should be grateful."

More silence, but I could hear his breathing, quick and shallow.

"What do I need to give you, Xavier?"

"I *will* kill them!"

"I know. Now quit thinking about what we want and what we are afraid of and start thinking about what *you* need. What is important for *you*, Xavier? What do *you want?*"

"I want, I need, *Jesus!* I need some coke, man!"

"Okay, we can do that, but try to focus. You need a car? You want to get out of state? You want a plane to Mexico? You need to start thinking about yourself for a change, man. You know, what about you? You are in a jam here, and you need to get somewhere safe. Right now, you hold all the aces. So it is time for you, Xavier Pereira, for once in your life, to say what *you* want!"

"Yeah." It sounded like he was thinking about what I'd said. "Yeah, yeahyeahyeah! Yeah, okay, right. I want a car. You gotta take me to the airport. I need a plane. One of them small, luxury models, with the leather seats, right? I gotta go to Mexico. To Los Mochis. And I don't want no one to fuckin' follow me there! I s-s-"

"You swear that, and I believe you. Now I am going to do that for you, Xavier." I dropped my voice. "I can promise you, Xavier, that there are people in New York right *now* who, politically, *really* just want you out of the equation. You understand me? What they really want is for the guy who is causing the trouble quietly to *go away*. You understand me? So work with me, dude. I will give you what you want, and we'll start with a good snort—"

"Yeah, yeah, right!"

"Then we'll get you a flight, and you'll need some cash, right? Don't go crazy, but maybe twenty grand—"

"Fifty!"

I sighed audibly. "I'll do my best. But I have to show something, dude. To show you are willing to play."

"Like what?"

"Like you swap the two women for me."

Dehan glared at me and mouthed silently but violently, *No! No way!*

Gordon gaped at me, and Mike walked away in disgust. Xavier was silent for a moment, then said, "No."

"Then I—"

"I want the girl."

"What?"

"I want the woman you were with. Detective Dehan. I want Detective Dehan."

TWELVE

"Detective Stone, can we go and talk, please?"

Dehan took my arm and led me away toward the Jaguar.

"So," she said under her breath as we walked, "it's okay for you to go in there and replace the hostages but not me?"

"It's out of the question. I'm not even going to discuss it. No. That's final."

"It's not your decision, Stone. Just like it wasn't my decision when you offered yourself."

We had reached the car, and I turned to face her. "Don't try and reason with me, Carmen—"

"Oh, I'm Carmen now, *John?*"

"You are not going in there to replace those hostages, and that is final, Dehan. It is not going to happen. If I have to knock you unconscious and resign from the PD, you are not going in there."

"But you are?"

"I don't care. It is just not going to happen."

Her face flushed with anger. "Why the hell not, Stone? What is this? The middle—"

"Because you are a woman!" She gaped. "And not only that, you are *my* woman! And I don't give a *damn* how unacceptable or primitive or *inappropriate* that is! That's how it is, and it is not going to change! If you go in there to replace those hostages, it will be over my dead body! And don't think I am exaggerating. I am not. You can divorce me, you can leave me, you can report me to the damned Woke Commission! If that's what it takes, so be it." I raised my voice and pointed at the squat. "*But you are not going into that building!*"

I turned to walk away but then turned back.

"That bastard is not going to hurt the woman I love, even if that means I lose you. Also, he does what he does to women. Not to men."

I walked back to Mike and the SWAT commander. I said, "He does what he does to women. Not to men. So a woman should not go in to replace the hostages. The object of this exercise is to get the women out of there, not put more women in. Especially women who arguably have a higher ransom value."

Mike sneered. "So what are you going to do, Romeo?"

I stared at him for five long, slow seconds. When he swallowed and looked away, I called Pereira.

"So?"

"No can do. The political risk is too high. They lose a cop and nobody cares. You do to a female cop what you did to Zeta, and the political price to pay is off the chart."

There was silence. Dehan was there staring into my eyes with no expression. Then Pereira's voice, like sandpaper, "She had it coming. She earned that. You don't—you d-d-d... You don't *fuckin'* divorce a guy when he's in jail! You don't—you don't— *You don't fuckin' tell him you're pregnant with another guy's fuckin' baby! When he's fuckin' behind bars, man!*"

I spoke without thinking. "Is that what brought you and Dave together?"

"*What?*"

"The stammer. Is that how you became friends?" His silence told me I'd nailed it. "Did he give you the idea, how you were going to kill her?"

His reply was quiet. "No... I mean, seein' him made me think about it. When I asked him, he said he never remembered doing it. Anyway, she had it coming."

"I agree."

"What the fuck would you know, cop?"

"We're wasting time. Every minute that passes, it gets more difficult for you to get out of here alive. Pretty soon, I'm going to be overruled, and they are going to storm in there and take you down. Let the girls go, take me in their place. You let me go at Los Mochis and I fly back to New York."

"I want Detective Dehan."

"It's not going to happen."

"Where's my coke? You said I could have some coke."

"Give me a straight answer, Pereira. I'll bring you a bag of coke. You let the girls go, and I come in with the coke. Then you get your car, your money, and your plane."

"You'll bring me the coke?"

"That's what I'm telling you."

"Dehan—"

I hung up and turned to the SWAT commander. "Captain. We're not ready to go in yet. But can you fire up your truck and move it closer to the main entrance without putting your men at risk?"

"Sure." He nodded and ran back to his men, issuing orders as he went. Thirty seconds later, the truck had fired up and was moving toward the entrance to the building, while armed men in helmets and flak jackets ran to the corner of the street to cover the windows at that side of the building.

My phone rang.

"What's happening? You said I'd be okay! You said you'd get me out of here! You said—"

"I *said* I need you to cooperate! Do you remember that part, Pereira? Do you remember the part where I said work with me? Do you remember I said show you are willing to play? *Do you remember that?*"

"Yes! Yes! For Chrissakes!"

"So understand this, Xavier! Act like a goddamn asshole and you get shot! Act smart and do as I say and you get to snort yourself to death in Mexico! *Do you understand?*"

I shouted the last question and was aware that I was not play-acting. I hung up and gave the commander the thumbs-up. He stopped moving but held his position. I turned to Gordon and pointed up the road.

"Hunts Point Avenue, next to the fried chicken, there's a pharmacy. I need talc and I need a transparent plastic bag. This is two hundred and fifty grams of coke I'm taking him. Okay? Go!"

"I have no car, Detective."

I threw her my keys, and her eyes went almost as wide as Dehan's. She spun and ran with her ponytail bouncing wildly, and a moment later, the Jag was roaring away, up the road, narrowly missing the chief's car as he turned into the street at the same corner.

When he climbed out of his vehicle, he didn't look happy.

"Will somebody tell me what's going on here?" He raised a hand to silence both me and Mike. "Carmen, brief me."

She made it brief and succinct, and left out the parts that were relevant only to her and me. She finished up, "Detective Stone made the point that it seems Pereira does what he does, so to speak, to women. So it would be counterproductive to replace his existing hostages with other women who would be, arguably, of a higher ransom value."

He frowned at me, raised an eyebrow, and muttered, "Fair point. I see you're still thinking on your feet. Was that Officer Gordon I saw escaping in your car?"

"Yes, sir. She has gone to get some talc."

"Cocaine." He turned to face me. "I can't authorize this, John. You know perfectly well that we do not negotiate with terrorists or criminals. Besides which, the moment you get off the plane in Los Mochis, Sinaloa will move in and either kill you or kidnap you for ransom, or most probably both."

I smiled. "I don't plan to go to Mexico, sir. We just need to get those girls out of there. Once the girls are out, you storm the place. You don't wait. You take them out and you move in. I'll keep him busy."

He turned to the commander. "Captain?"

He nodded. "We can do it. Pull the girls out, and as they are removed from the risk area, we throw in a couple of flashbangs—"

I was shaking my head. "That's going to put me out of commission for a couple of hours at least. I need to be functional when I get out of there." I shook my head again. "The minute the girls are out, I am going to kick him in the nuts so hard he'll be singing soprano for the San Francisco Opera for the next ten years. You move in. I want him alive, though. I *need* him alive."

People began to move. My Jag turned in at the top of the drive. Dehan was kneeling beside me, unstrapping something from her leg. Mike spoke to the chief.

"Sir, I'd like to be removed from this case."

The chief glanced at him. "Done. See me in my office back at the station." He moved off to talk to the SWAT commander, and I followed Mike toward his RAM.

"Mike—"

He stopped beside his vehicle and turned to face me. I took a fistful of his shirt collar in my left hand and thrust my face into his. There was a hot rage in my belly that was fogging my head. I spoke very quietly.

"You go home, you get your wife, you bring her here, and you put her in there with that sadistic bastard for him to cut her belly open and let her bleed to death. When you've done that, you piece of shit, you look me in the eye and call me Romeo again. We are not done."

I shoved him back against his truck and returned to where Dehan was watching me. As I walked, I noticed something flapping at my ankle. I looked down and saw it was a small holster half strapped to my calf. As I approached her, I said, "What's this...?"

She was still hunkered down. "Sig Sauer, P365. Five point eight inches in length, one inch width, weighs less than eighteen ounces. You have it on your ankle. While he's opening the talc and the girls are running, you shoot him in the knee."

"What would I do without you?"

She finished strapping on the holster and shoved in the piece. Then she stood and leaned in so her nose was an eighth of an inch from my chin.

"You came damned close to finding out today, pardner. But you know what? I thought of a better punishment." She narrowed her eyes, smiled, and snarled in a deeply disturbing way. "You ain't *never* going to find out, you damned caveman!"

The chief approached. "You ready, Stone?"

"Yeah, as I'll ever be."

"Good. You call him, you tell him you're coming over, he must have the women ready, and you'll take him the goods. The car is on its way, and the jet is fueling up."

I looked around and found Gordon. She was approaching with a transparent plastic bag heavily taped. You could just make out it was full of white powder. She handed it to me, took a deep breath, and said, "Sir, Detective, Chief, I would like to volunteer for this if he wants a woman to go."

I smiled at her. "Don't be in such a hurry, Gordon. You're doing fine. We don't want any women hostages in there. Stand by."

I pulled out my cell. It rang once.

"Stone?"

"Yeah, it's me. Now you listen, this goes down one way or they pull the plug. You listening?"

"Yeah, don't threaten me."

"You want to make it to Los Mochis alive you will relax and listen."

"I'm listening."

"I have two hundred and fifty grams of coke for you here. I am unarmed. I'm going to walk to the front door in my shirt sleeves so you can see I have no weapon. I will be carrying the coke. You got it so far?"

"I ain't stupid. You come to the door, you got coke, and you don't got no weapon. What next?"

"You can stay inside where our marksmen can't see you. You can keep me lined up. You let the girls go. Once they are outside and safe, I will come in with the coke."

"I don't like it."

"What's the prob—"

"How do I know when I let the girls go, how do I know you won't just run? Then what've I got?"

The chief, the commander, Gordon, and Dehan were all staring at me. I gave a small sigh.

"You're not listening, Pereira. I'll be just inside the door. If I try to run, you can take me. I won't stand a chance."

"No. This is how we do it. You stand inside the doorway. Behind you, you got a car ready to take me to Teterboro. I take the girls as far as the door. When I got you six feet away, you get in the car, behind the wheel, and I get in behind you. Anything goes wrong, you die."

I looked at the chief. He nodded.

"Okay, you got it. Give me a few minutes to get a car." I hung up and looked at the SWAT commander. "You'd better have your best man ready, Captain. I want him alive, but I want to be alive to take him down."

"You got it, Detective."

He said that, but I knew it was not an ideal setup, by any stretch of the imagination. The only place he could put his shooter and his backup was in an empty lot opposite the door to the building. The door was three foot across, it would be dark on the inside and occupied by three people they did not want to shoot, and one target who was in shadow. And most of the time I would be blocking that target.

In addition, according to Pereira's new instructions, there would now be a car between him and the shooters too.

The chief said, "I want officers either side of the door to get those women out of harm's way." Gordon's hand went up. Dehan took her away and five minutes later I saw Dehan against the wall to the left of the door, and Gordon on the right. Then the car arrived. It was an anonymous-looking gray Honda. The driver parked across the door, got out and moved quickly to safety behind the patrol cars.

I pulled my cell, the chief gave me the nod and I called. I spoke before he did.

"OK, Pereira, no more delays. The moment the media get hold of this the deal is off and you get shot. Are we on the same page?"

"You got the car?"

"The car is parked out front. I've got your coke." I started walking. "I am walking to the doorway now. You bring out the girls and let them go. Try to make some smart choices for once in your life, OK? And maybe you'll come out of this in one piece."

His voice came back as a rasp. "Don't threaten me, Stone."

"Just be smart, Xavier. Nobody wants this to play out right more than I do. Just stay cool and be smart." I reached the doorway and stopped two feet from the entrance. "I'm here."

He hung up, and I put my cell in my back pocket. The door stood open, but all I could see was an oblong tunnel of darkness. Then there was a thin slash of light, vertical from floor to ceiling. There was a jumbled movement of shadows, some whimpering and sobbing. Then the shadows were moving toward me, growing in the darkness. Shevron's pale sobbing face emerged from the gloom. Sandy was behind her, looking just as pale and sick, but controlling her weeping. They were moving toward me fast, and behind them, looking crazy, was Pereira, with a pistol pointed straight at my head.

THIRTEEN

He half screamed, "*Gimme the coke!*"

I stepped aside so Sandy and Shevron could get by. They were running, pushing to get past, and Shevron was screaming. I was aware out of the side of my eye of Dehan grabbing Sandy and dragging her running toward the safety of the cars. Then Pereira was on me, thrusting the weapon in my face and screaming at me, "In the car! Get in the car! Behind the wheel! Gimme the fucking coke!"

He was big and heavy, and he was thrusting the muzzle of his weapon in my face. I backed up a step without thinking, and he was out in the street, pushing me toward the car. I couldn't see behind me, but I knew Shevron had had to run around the hood or the trunk to get to safety. I glanced and didn't see Gordon, and in a fraction of a second I knew what had happened. Shevron was out in the open and Gordon had gone after her to pull her to safety. My belly burned and my heart thumped hard high up in my chest.

Pereira looked past me, and what he must have seen was a running cop going after Shevron. He leveled his weapon. I heard myself scream some inarticulate noise. I rushed him, grabbing for the gun, trying to force it up. The air exploded twice. My vision was filled with his crimson, twisted face. I didn't think. I drove my right fist into his floating ribs in a tight, vicious hook, followed an instant later by my left into his liver. He doubled up, vomiting. I didn't pause. I drove a second right hook into his head, and he fell to the ground.

My ears were ringing from the two shots, and I was unsteady on my feet. I reached for his weapon, turned, and stumbled against the car. All I could see was uniforms running, a milling crowd. I found Dehan over on my right. She had her arms around Sandy, who was struggling and screaming silently. Everything was silent. Everyone was running and shouting, but all I could hear was a high-pitched ringing.

I made my way around the hood. The chief was moving toward me, talking. Past him, I could see Dehan running. All in silence. I ejected the magazine from the weapon and engaged the safety. I handed it to the chief. He was staring at me, his lips moving. Dehan had my arm in her hands. I looked away from them both at the group on the ground. The SWAT commander was kneeling beside Gordon. There was blood on the road. Beside her, Shevron's hair was matted red. Her mouth was gaping. Her eyes were open but unseeing.

I swallowed, like I could unblock my ears that way. I pointed back at the car behind me. "Pereira," I said but didn't hear my own voice. Dehan turned away and called to someone through the silence. I put my hands to my ears to try to stop the ringing. A guy in a uniform acknowledged Dehan and came toward us. Dehan went behind me, and I watched her move around the hood of the car, to the entrance to the building. A uniform had my arm and was mouthing at me. I pointed at Dehan.

"*Help her with Pereira. Cuff him.*"

He mouthed at me, *I can hear you.*

Then his eyes and his smile shifted. I followed his gaze. Pereira was rising, like a filthy shadow unfolding from the ground. Dehan had cuffs in her hands as she approached, and her face said she was shouting. The uniform who was with me reached for his weapon and went to join her. I was shouting in a silent void. Because I could see him reaching behind his back, to his waistband. Dehan rushed him, but he was fast, and the next moment he had a semi-automatic in his left hand pointed straight at my head. Dehan froze.

I went to move, but the next instant he was pointing the weapon at Dehan's belly. He was laughing and talking, but I couldn't hear what he was saying. I could see the left side of his face, purple and swelling, and blood on his chin. But I couldn't hear him.

Dehan was looking at me for a signal. I ignored her because the more he was aware of our connection, the greater the danger to her.

He backed up. The gun was pointing at me again. He was talking to Dehan, pointing at the car. He was telling her to get behind the wheel. I yelled, "*No!*" and turned my back on them, screaming at the marksmen, "*Take him out! Take him out!*"

I turned back and Dehan was behind the wheel. He was climbing in behind her, with the semi pressed up against the back of the seat. Then the car was moving, taking the corner into Gilbert Place, accelerating away, and I was running, hollering, screaming, in silence.

Then I was running; not after the car but back to my Jag to go after them. But everywhere I went, there were men and women in uniform blocking my way, grabbing me, holding me, dragging me back. Then there was the chief, holding my face, shouting at me, and slowly, painfully, his voice filtered through the ringing silence.

"*John! John! Listen to me! Look at me! Look at my eyes! We-have-a-chopper-on-them!*"

I stopped struggling. The grief was a physical thing that was tearing at me inside. But I knew I would be useless to Dehan if I went to pieces. I had to hold it together until I got her back.

The cops around me started to let go. At the end of Faile Street, I could see lights: two ambulances arriving and Frank's ancient Ford Estate. A huge swell of emotion, like a dark, dense wave in a cold harbor, threatened to overwhelm me. Thoughts: dangerous thoughts, questions, what would I be? What would I become? What would life be...?

I fought down the feeling, silenced the questions. The chief was in front of me, peering into my face. "You have a chopper on them?"

He nodded. "Yes, can you hear me?"

The ringing was subsiding, but he still sounded like he was talking through cotton wool. "Yeah, barely."

"We have a tracking device on the car. We have a chopper following them."

I pointed at the ambulances that had pulled up behind him. "I need to have the medic check my ears. Then I need to go after them."

"No way, John."

I stepped in close to him and placed my hand on his shoulder. "If you forbid it, then I'll have to break the law and lose my pension, sir. Nobody knows Dehan the way I do. Nobody knows what to expect from her except me. Nobody will be as useful as I will. Hook me up to the chopper. It will be best all around. Sir."

There must have been something in my eyes or in my voice because he didn't argue. He nodded briefly and said, "Let's go see the doc."

We passed Shevron. Her face and body had been covered. Gordon was on a gurney. Her eyes were open, but she looked groggy, and her pupils were the size of soup plates. She frowned at me, and I stepped over and took her hand. I couldn't hear her, but I read her lips. She said, "Sorry, Detective. I screwed up."

I clamped my teeth hard and got that weird burn you get in your nose when tears are threatening to spill. I couldn't say anything, but I smiled at her and gave her hand a squeeze. I made a grating noise which sounded something like, "You did good," and they wheeled her away into an ambulance.

I saw Frank climb out of his station wagon. He was peering at me as he slammed the door. The chief and a paramedic made me sit in the back of an ambulance as Frank approached.

"What happened?"

I said, "Nothing," and had to repeat it because I didn't know if I'd said it too loud or too quiet. "Pereira fired his gun while I was gripping his wrist. I'm partially deaf." I jerked my head at where Shevron was lying on the black asphalt. "It was worse for Shevron and Gordon."

"Turn your head and shut up." He shone a small flashlight into my ear and said, "Can you hear anything at all?"

"I could hear better if you took the cotton wool out of your mouth. Fifteen minutes ago, I could hear nothing but ringing. Now I can make out what you're saying, but it's not very clear."

"It'll wear off in the next few hours. If you're lucky, it will wear off completely in a day or so. Get Carmen to—"

"Carmen has been abducted."

Frank stared at me for a beat, then turned to the chief. The chief said, "We have a chopper…"

I cut him short. "I need to be tuned in to the chopper. I need to be going after them. I need to do that now."

Frank said, "I need to get on. Keep me posted."

He turned away and went and hunkered down beside Shevron. I looked at the chief. "He'll head south. He'll dump the car and steal another. When night falls, he can shake the chopper. When he dumps the car, Dehan will become baggage, and he'll kill her."

"But what can you do, John?"

"I don't know," I snarled. "But if she gets killed while I am sitting around waiting…"

He closed his eyes and sighed. "All right. You can't take your Jaguar. He'll spot it immediately."

"Same applies to a patrol car. We haven't got time to wait for an unmarked. This has to be now, sir."

"You take my Charger. I'll take yours back to the station.

There are vehicles in pursuit right now. You stay behind them and let them do their job. You understand?"

"Yes, sir. Thank you."

I didn't wait. I gave him my keys, and he gave me his fob, and two minutes later, I was listening to the chopper's communication as it followed Pereira's car along I-95 into New Jersey and south toward Philadelphia.

I surged onto Hunts Point Avenue leaning on the horn, made a right, and thundered onto the Sheridan Expressway, closing on eighty miles per hour. I had a lot of distance to make up, and I knew that Dehan would be driving too fast for him to do anything to her. If the car is going a hundred MPH, you don't shoot the driver. That was good, but like I said, it meant I had a lot of distance to make up.

I screamed around the ramp at the bus depot doing sixty and catapulted out onto I-95, where I began to make some serious speed. I was lucky. There was not much traffic, and I could put my foot down. I prayed for some kind of spooky, action-at-a-distance telepathy so Dehan would know to go fast but slow enough for me to catch up. I was doing one-forty. If she kept it to a hundred, I'd be closing on her at forty miles per hour.

A hundred and forty miles per hour is terrifying, but I didn't give a damn. There was only one thing clear in my mind, and that was that I had to reach her and get between Pereira and her before he did anything. Because there was no doubt in my mind at all that he intended to hurt her. As long as I was alive, as long as I was breathing, as long as there was living blood in my veins, that could not happen.

The radio crackled as I hit the George Washington Bridge.

"Target vehicle is at Ridgefield Park, following I-95 south."

If she was at Ridgefield, that put five or six miles between us, which meant I'd catch up to them in less than ten minutes. At a rough guess, I figured I'd close on them at Newark on the Turnpike.

I saw the needle climbing toward one-fifty. I was over the

bridge and screaming south, approaching cars that were doing seventy and eighty miles per hour as though they were stationary.

The radio crackled, and a voice said, "We have a Dodge Charger approaching the target vehicle. We clock him at one hundred and fifty miles per hour. He is approaching the target vehicle at fifty miles per hour. We estimate contact in two to three minutes."

He wasn't wrong. A minute later, I had them ahead of me, and I was closing fast. I began to slow until I was beside them, matching their speed. I could see Dehan through the window. She looked cool and relaxed, but it was a cool and relaxed I knew well. Under that surface, I knew she was burning.

Pereira was behind her, screaming. He lowered the window, stretched out his arm with the weapon in it, and pulled off a shot. I braked slightly as the gun flashed.

I reached down and pulled the Sig from the ankle holster, then closed in until my front wheel was level with his rear door. I could see him shifting, moving, trying to get a bead on me. I steadied the car so we were maybe three or four inches apart.

The risk of hitting Dehan was high. But the risk of not stopping him now was higher. The angle was right, and if I stayed steady, any strays would go out into the wasteland by the airfield. I put six rounds into the back, nice and steady, through the glass and through the bodywork.

Her car began to slow, her hazard lights flashing. I hit my hazards too and let her move ahead. Ninety, eighty, fifty, and we cruised to a stop. I was out before she stopped, running with the 365 in my right hand, reaching with my left for the back door. I wrenched it open. He was lying on the seat, drenched in blood, weeping. I took his weapon from the floor. Dehan was on her phone. "...request backup and an ambulance."

She got out, shoving her phone in her back pocket. She grinned at me, came real close, and yelled, "*What took you so long? Can you hear me, Stone?*"

Then she put her arms around me and squeezed so hard it hurt. But it felt good.

The chopper was circling overhead. The traffic was giving us a wide berth and, according to Dehan, there were sirens audible in the distance. She grabbed some reflective triangles from the trunk of the chief's Charger and, while she was placing them, I leaned on the open window from which Pereira had shot at me and studied him stretched out. After a moment, I called Dehan, and she came and stood beside me.

I said,

"We caught the guy who killed Zeta. The killing had a motive, the oldest motive in the book, jealousy. But this guy did not kill Elaine Gallardo or any of the others."

She stared at me. "How can you know that?"

I reached down and grabbed his foot and heaved it onto the window. She shifted her stare to the cheap sneaker, and I said, "Size thirteen."

FOURTEEN

We were in the chief's office back at the station house. Dehan was sitting on the sofa under the bonsai which sat on the windowsill. I was in a chair against the wall and Mike was standing leaning against the door with his arms crossed. The chief was saying,

"John, I have to agree that the size of his feet, set against everything else we know, does seem rather thin. As Mike has pointed out, it is far from impossible to leave size nine footprints even if you are a size thirteen, or any other size, for that matter. I mean, we are not saying that Xavier Pereira was the Castle Hill Ripper, but merely that he became friends with him and became a copycat. We know this to be the case."

I let him trail off before I answered.

"Sir, with all due respect, that is piggybacking. What we know is that Pereira and Dave Clark met and talked at Attica. He even admitted that Clark inspired him in how to kill Zeta. That is an established fact, but establishing *that* fact does not establish A, that Pereira became a copycat, B, that he killed Elaine Gallardo, or, most important of all, that Dave Clark was the Ripper in the first place."

Mike rolled his eyes elaborately and groaned. "This again. He *confessed!* The jury found him *guilty!* G-I-L-T-E."

I tried hard to ignore him and his spelling. I kept my eyes on the chief.

"Sir, as you have said from the beginning, there are serious reasons to doubt both Clark's guilt and the validity of his confession."

"Like what?" It was Mike again. I kept my eyes on the chief. He looked embarrassed.

"Talk us through them, John."

"Yeah, John, talk us through them."

"The first point is that it is extremely unlikely that any woman would open the door to either Dave Clark or Xavier Pereira at night in the Bronx. We are talking about two men who are big and look very menacing. Yet all seven of the victims opened the door and allowed the killer to enter while they closed the door behind them and then joined them in the middle of the floor. This happened in every case and suggests very strongly that when they looked through the peephole, they saw a person who was *not* menacing, was welcome and possibly familiar."

"Yeah." It was Mike again. "Or somebody holding a wad of cash."

"Sir, there is nothing to suggest that all the victims were prostitutes, and could you please ask Detective Romano to keep his mouth shut unless he has something useful to say?"

The chief scowled at Mike. "Do, please, stop interrupting, Detective. You will get a chance to answer in a moment."

I went on, "So my first point is that both Clark and Pereira are intimidating-looking men, and the victims would be unlikely to open the door to either of them. The second point is that these murders were carried out in a very precise, meticulous manner with a great deal of attention to detail and forethought. The covering of the shoes, the shower, the notebooks, the fact that every murder was committed in precisely the same way on almost identical dates. The behavior is almost ritualistic, very carefully planned and executed."

"Now Stone is an FBI profiler!"

"Neither of these two men has the intelligence or the temperament to plan and execute a murder—much less a series of murders—in that way. Zeta was murdered in a fit of jealous rage. Yes, he stabbed her in the belly and made the classic L-shaped cut. But any violent criminal who uses a knife knows that that is the disemboweling cut. It was the only aspect of the murder which matched the Ripper. There were no footprints, there was no shower, the body was removed from the site of the crime, God only knows what he was planning to do, but that itself tells us he was out of control and had no plan. And in addition to this, sir, it came just a few hours after Elaine Gallardo. But Pereira had known even while he was in prison that Zeta was pregnant. So why did he go and kill Gallardo in his usual, meticulous style, and a few hours later go all barbarian on Zeta? It makes no sense." I looked at Mike. "You know, no S-E-N-S."

The chief cleared his throat. "So what are you suggesting? Carmen?"

She sat forward with her elbows on her knees. "Yeah, we are suggesting that the Ripper framed Clark." Mike made a snorting noise like an aborted laugh. "He certainly showed the intelligence to plan an effective frame. He took a year's break during 2022, just as he did in 2019, and now he is back. And if we don't find him, he will kill again in November. But we are not looking for a big, brutish Neanderthal. We are looking for somebody who is a good planner, somebody who is not threatening, somebody who is helpful and gives the impression of being warm and kind, even if inside he is cold and devoid of compassion."

Mike gestured at her with an open hand. "Sir, do I have to listen to this? I know what they are doing. They're setting up a frame."

The chief screwed up his brow. "Excuse me?"

"It's what it amounts to, sir. They have decided that Harry Panayotes—"

"Who, now?"

"His name is Hercules Panayotes, but his pals call him Harry. He manages the Shoprite on the Boulevard. And these two clowns—"

"Detective Romano! That is *enough!*"

"I'm sorry, sir. These two *detectives* have decided that he is the Ripper."

The chief looked at me. "Is this true, John?"

"He is among our persons of interest, sir. We are certainly not aiming to frame him, but he does have a number of the attributes we'd expect, plus he runs the geographical spot which was the acknowledged center of the Ripper's activities. He is an extremely good organizer, he is very popular with his customers, he knew all the victims by name, and they knew him, and he is apparently a very warm, friendly person, though according to his employees, he can be pretty ruthless. I know for a fact he believes that what he calls whores deserve what they get. Apparently, he is not alone in that view."

Dehan finished off for me. "But what Detective Stone has just said is a very long way from having decided he is guilty. What is true is that he is a *much* better fit than Clark—who, incidentally, *he* would have been in a perfect position to frame."

The chief stared down at his desk for a good few seconds, then looked up at Mike.

"Why was this Hercules Panayotes not investigated?"

"Because what they are saying is stupid, sir. I've known Harry for years. There is no way—"

"Detective Romano, you are suspended effective immediately pending an investigation into your handling of the Ripper case. Kindly hand me your weapon and your badge. You will make available to Detectives Stone and Dehan all your files and notes. John, Carmen, you have this case. Detective Romano. You may leave, but do not leave the city, and make yourself available over the next days for questioning."

It took him about fifteen seconds, which if you count them out is a long time, then he stepped forward and dropped his badge and his gun on the desk. After that, he turned and walked out, slamming the door behind him.

When he was gone, the chief asked, "How serious are you about this Hercules?"

Dehan answered. "Mixed, sir. Like we said, he fits the profile we are making, plus he is the guy Zeta left Pereira for. One minute that convinces me he's the guy, the next minute it convinces me he ain't."

I clarified. "Mr. Panayotes makes a distinction between prostitutes, whom he considers working women, and what he calls whores, who offer their sexuality in exchange for favors like rent, food, etcetera. How Zeta fit into that view, we don't know yet. Maybe he had no idea about her professional background. We need to talk to him."

He grunted. "Be tactful. He may be perfectly innocent. Approach him perhaps on the pretext of informing him and couch your questions as though you are investigating her death as opposed to the Ripper case. Of course, his alibis, at this stage..."

"Gordon was looking into that."

He gave another grunt. "I hope you are clear that what happened to Shevron and Officer Gordon was in no way your fault, John."

"I am not clear on that yet, sir. I need to think it through. I should have been more aware of Sandy and Shevron's possible movements around the car, I should have briefed Gordon more thoroughly..."

"She was a trained officer, John. Shevron was running for cover, and Gordon should have known not to run into Pereira's line of fire. She was brave, but what she did was foolish. Nobody is holding you responsible, except perhaps yourself."

"Thank you, sir." I glanced at Dehan. "Perhaps we should go talk to Panayotes."

She nodded, and we rose. At the door, the chief asked, "How's your hearing? You want to take the rest of the day to rest?"

"I beg your pardon, sir? I didn't hear you."

He smiled. I smiled back, and we left.

Outside, late afternoon was damp copper with broken clouds, and the shadows were deep. We drove slowly and in silence to the parking lot at the store and pushed through the big glass doors. There was a security guard by the door looking bored. I showed him my badge.

"Detective John Stone. We need to see Mr. Panayotes."

"You just missed him, Detectives. He left for home about fifteen minutes ago. You want me to call him for you?"

I shook my head. "That's fine. We'll find him."

As I was turning to leave, I saw a guy approaching from within the store. He was smiling and raised a hand in greeting. It took me a moment to register.

"Good afternoon, Detectives. How's the investigation?"

I pointed at him and thought for a moment. "Oliver."

"Yes, sir. Can I help you guys in any way? I'm just on my way home."

"Where's home?"

"Lafayette? Just by the church. Mom was adamant. She would not move to New York unless she could be walking distance of her church."

"She sounds like an interesting lady." I nodded to the security guard and moved for the door, speaking as I went. "No, we came to see Mr. Panayotes, but it seems he's gone already."

"Yup, he's home by now. Poor guy's been a bit off color the last couple of days."

Dehan looked interested. "Yeah, how's that?"

We paused by the Jag, and he frowned and shrugged. "Well, he's not the nicest guy in the world at the best of times. But I get that. It's his job, he has thousands of customers, and he needs to be on top of things. I understand that. But he is always real charming with the customers, and he is a definite asset to the shop. So I actually have a lot of respect for him. But the last couple of days, he's been sullen, angry, rude to the customers, which is like, unheard of. Something's on his mind."

I said, "Can we drop you somewhere?"

His face colored, and he laughed. "Oh, lord, I hate to be rude, but if my mother sees me getting out of a police car, there'll be hell to pay!"

I laughed and pointed to the Jag. "She'll never know."

His face lit up. "Oh, cool! A Jaguar Mark II. That's one of the great classics. Well ahead of its time."

I opened the door for him, and he climbed in back. I got behind the wheel, and Dehan got in beside me. "You interested in classic cars?" I asked as I fired her up.

"Not really, but Mr. Panayotes was talking 'bout buying a classic car recently. He said he wanted a Jaguar, but a classic from before they were taken over by Ford. He was between the Mark II and the later S-Type." He laughed. "Which was partly a Ford project."

Dehan asked, "Why the classic car?"

"He said he was going to come into some money. And when he did, he was going to buy a Jag. He always wanted one, since he was a kid in Greece."

I laughed. "I wanted one since I was a kid in the Bronx."

He was sitting between us on the back seat, leaning forward.

"We never really had much use for a car back home. We had the old Chevy truck for a while." He smiled. "Mom inherited some land from her dad, and we were going to move there and run the farm, but she had to sell it."

Dehan shifted in her seat. "Was that when you moved here?"

"No, long before. I was just a kid. She always had to work real hard. So when I was old enough, I told her, 'Come on, Ma, we're moving somewhere where I can make some money and look after you.' And that's what we did."

Dehan smiled. These were the stories she loved. Stories about family and loyal kids. "When was that?" she said.

"Oh, let me see, that would have been…" His gaze was lost, past Dehan at the passing street. "…early in 2020, February 2020. It was cold, but nothing like the cold back home. We'd found that nice house on Lafayette and moved in and made our home here." He pointed ahead. "That green one on the right." I pulled over. "That was mighty kind of you. You want to come in for coffee and meet Mom?"

"Maybe some other time, Oliver. Listen, before you go, this is strictly unofficial, between us—"

His laugh was bright and short, with bright amused eyes. "Does that exist with police officers? Your duty is to the law. I am happy to answer any questions you have, Detective Dehan, but I don't believe they will be unofficial or between us!"

He laughed again, and Dehan arched an eyebrow at him.

"Nobody likes a wiseass, kid. Not even one from North Dakota. But yeah, you're right. Nothing is strictly unofficial. What we are interested in is Mr. Panayotes' relationships with his customers."

He became serious and looked down at his hands between his knees.

"I have to tell you I am not comfortable talking about my employer. It seems very disloyal."

I shifted in my seat to get a better look at him. "What we want, Oliver, is to eliminate him as a suspect. Ideally, we would have alibis for him going back to 2018, but for reasons which don't concern us now, that didn't happen. So we need to get whatever background we can. If he is guilty, then he should not be protected. If he is innocent, your information will help clear him."

"I guess." But he didn't look happy. "I can't tell you anything about 2018 or 2019. I was still in my teens and living at home. But

I'll give your question some thought." He hesitated. "I honestly have to say, Mr. Panayotes is big and noisy and very demanding of his workers. But he is basically a good, kind man."

I handed him my card. "Call me later or tomorrow. Don't think too long. Girls are dying, and so are unborn babies."

He frowned at me and after a moment took the card. "I'll call you this evening, when I've given it some thought."

He slid across the seat and opened the door. There he paused and gave me the frown again. "Is this what happens to human beings when they become urbanized? They turn on each other?"

I didn't answer. He slid out, slammed the door, and made his way through his white picket gate to the front of his green, clapboard-gabled house.

I pulled away and headed north at a leisurely pace toward Bruckner Boulevard. After a while, I glanced at Dehan. She was staring fixedly ahead. I said, "Is it? Is it what happens to people when you pile them into gigantic hives? They lose their humanity?"

"I don't know, Stone." She was quiet for another while as we crossed Westchester Creek. Then, "But I can't shake the thought. What if I had been pregnant today? What if I was pregnant now?"

I stared at her and raised my eyebrows. "Are you?"

She laughed. "No." Then she shrugged. "Well, I don't think so. We haven't been especially careful, have we?"

"No," I said after a while, wondering why.

FIFTEEN

WE PULLED UP OUTSIDE PANAYOTES' HOUSE. HIS CAR was in the drive, outside the garage, the way he said he left it when he was going out again. I left the Jag across his trunk, so he couldn't reverse, and we climbed out.

Dehan rang the bell while I looked around. The house was one-story, free-standing, and surrounded by lawn. Dehan rang again, and after a minute, the door opened a few inches, and Panayotes peered out.

"Detectives." It was a statement, like he'd detected us in a petri dish. His shoulders rose an eighth of an inch, and he made a face like constipation. "Is not good time."

I came up behind Dehan. "Is it ever, Hercules?"

Another tiny shrug. His hair was disheveled, and his eyes were swollen. "Now is worse than usual."

Dehan said, "We really need to talk to you, Mr. Panayotes. And I am pretty sure you don't want to have this conversation out here."

He grunted, closed the door, and opened it again a moment later. He looked a mess. He was barefoot, his shirt was undone and untucked, and through the open door to the living room, I could see a bottle of Scotch on the coffee table. Beside the bottle, there was a glass with a liberal measure in it.

Dehan thrust her hands in her pockets and gave him a once-over. "You don't look like a happy man, Mr. Panayotes. Something troubling you?"

Another shrug, slightly larger. "Nah, is private matter."

"Are you sure?" I pointed to the living room. "Shall we go in and sit down?"

He didn't look like the idea thrilled him, but he gestured us in and followed.

"You want drink?"

Dehan shook her head. I said, "No, thanks." He sat on the sofa, and we took the chairs either side, at right angles to him. Dehan jerked her chin at the bottle. "Long day?"

He didn't answer. He shifted his gaze to me. I asked him, "Do you know a woman by the name of Zeta Reticuli?"

He covered his face and groaned. After a long moment, he said, "Where is she? What has she tell you about me?"

I glanced at Dehan. Her eyebrows twitched. I said, "It's time to come clean, Hercules."

His hands slipped halfway down his face so his big, bloodshot eyes were gazing at me.

"This woman is a liar," he said. "She lies all the time. She lies professionally. She is a whore. One-big-whore!"

He dropped his hands to his knees and started weeping noisily. It was a curious uninhibited, unselfconscious flood of emotion. He turned his gaze on Dehan, holding out a hand toward her, splayed palm-up, wide open. "You know what she tell me? She tell me she is an *actress!* And I believe her. *An actress!*"

He sat erect, sliding his palms up his body, looking left and right like a bird. "She is elegant, she is beautiful, she has the culture. Of course I believe her. And she comes, two three times in the week, talking to me, 'Oh, Mr. Pany this, oh Mr. Pany that,' nothing, nothing is too much trouble for me with this magnificent woman!"

He buried his face in his hands again, shaking his head. After a moment, he raised his face again. It was wet, and he made a sound like the last dregs of water going down a drain. "Finally, *finally* I am find the courage and I say to her, 'Zeta'"—he pronounced it 'theta'—"Zeta, you will please have dinner with me." He made an expansive gesture with his hand encompassing everything. "I will pay for everything! You will please be my guest?" He leaned forward, toward Dehan. "Do you think she said yes?" Before she could answer, he closed his eyes and shook his head. "No! She says to me, 'My dear Mr. Pany, I would love to say yes. But I am a lady, and I cannot go with a married man.'"

He raised both hands up to God. "This, I tell myself, is a lady! Not a whore, but a lady."

He sat nodding silently so long I finally asked him, "Well, what about your wife, Hercules? Does she live permanently with her mother?"

He raised his eyes only to regard me. His expression reminded me of a bloodhound.

"I have no wife. I tell everybody I have a wife, but I have no wife."

Dehan asked, "Could you please explain that, Mr. Panayotes?"

"People expect a man like me to be married. I am a figure in the community. Many people know me. Many women know me. If I am not married, they wonder why." He put his head on one side and spread his hands wide. "They think I am maybe *poústis*, going with other men. And sometimes women who are married are wanting to complicate my life, 'Oh Mr. Pany, I come and make the dinner for you, I bring you some apple pie.' Simple solution. I am married."

"But you're not married."

"No."

"Have you ever been married?"

"No. I have no time for married. And women always making problems. Better I live alone, and if I need…"—he made a vulgar gesture—"Eh? Eh? I pick up the telephone, and in half an hour I have a wife for fifteen minutes, and she goes home and leave me in peace."

I said, "That's a prostitute, not a whore."

"Exactly."

I nodded. "But you decided that Zeta—"

"Oh, Zeta, Zeta, Zeta! How she is break my heart!"

Dehan asked him, "What happened?"

"I never go her house. Everybody knows me in Castle Hill. If the women see me goin' into Zeta's house, they begin to gossip. This I cannot have. So always she is comin' to my house. Discreet, elegant, a lady."

"So what happened?"

"It makes a week, little bit more than a week, I am tell myself in my office, 'I will tell her to marry me!' I am so happy that day. I know she will say yes. So after work I am take my car and go to her house. I don't care! If people see me, I don't care! Because I am going to marry this woman for myself! I ring on her door, she is so happy to see me, I have flowers for her. She take me into her elegant living room, and she make me one martini. She say, 'Pany, I have some news to tell you.' 'Oh,' I say to her, 'I have something to ask you.' 'Well,' she say to me, 'I think better I go first.' 'Of course!'" He held out both hands and nodded magnanimously. "'Of course, you go first.' She says just one moment and she is going upstairs. She goes."

He made a small gesture with his hands, as though propelling her upstairs.

"And while I am waiting—I have never seen this house before. I have never been inside this house before!—I see the television. And next to the television I am seeing like a bookcase, but with movies. Romantic movies because she is a woman. *Harry Meet Sally, Four Weddings and the Funeral, Titanic*..." He trailed off, nodding. "And then I see more films, DVDs, and I see the name Zeta Reticuli. 'Oh!' I think, I am happy, I see now a movie with my woman!"

His face twisted, flushed red, and he bellowed as he slammed his fist down on the table, sending his glass flying. "*She is whore! She is filthy whore! Makin' filthy porno movies! My wife is whore!*"

He fell back into the sofa, covering his face and sobbing noisily. After a moment, he sat upright and spread his hands.

"I am sitting, staring, I cannot believe. And she comes in, standing in the open door. She sees the movie in my hand, and she laughs. 'Oh you found those,' she say to me. 'We can watch one later if you want. But first I have to tell you...' and she hold up a stick. A stick! 'I am pregnant, Pany. And you are the daddy.'"

Dehan winced and muttered, "Man..."

"I shout, I shout like a crazy man, I call her a whore, a bitch, I go crazy, a miracle that I do not kill her there, right there, but to stop me from this, I go!"

I frowned. "You left."

"I left. Because if I don't left, I kill her. So I am go. Left. In my car and drive like crazy man. She is crying, crying like a child."

I sighed. "Was that the last time you heard from her?"

"She call me many times that day and next day. I do not answering her. I block her number."

"Mr. Panayotes, Hercules, I'm afraid I have some bad news for you."

He didn't seem to hear. He reached out both hands toward me, staring with weeping eyes. "I am thinkin' I should forgive. Maybe I can forgive. She done this long time ago. And the baby. Who is gonna look after the baby? I can help her, and give baby a good home. Is my baby!"

"Harry!" He stopped dead at the name. "I have some very bad news for you. I am so sorry, but Zeta is dead, and so is the baby."

The room was very quiet. He was frowning hard, like I had spoken to him in another language he didn't understand. Dehan was watching him. I was trying to read his face. All the emotion had gone, all the turbulence and noisy madness. There was just a still, quiet frown.

"Dead?"

"Yes, I'm afraid so."

His mouth was trying to form words. He gestured with his hand in the direction of her house. "But I saw her..."

"A week ago."

"She was alive." He frowned at the floor, looking this way and that, like he might have left the explanation lying down there. "How? How does this happen?"

I gave Dehan a glance, but she had caught it too. After a moment, she said, "What is it you don't understand, Mr. Panayotes?"

I said, "You didn't kill her."

Still the uncomprehending frown. "No, I did not kill her."

"But you thought for a moment maybe you did?"

"No."

Dehan asked him, "What about the whores, Mr. Panayotes?"

"The whores..." He said it to the rug under his feet. And again, "The whores..."

"They seem to be a big deal to you."

"Everywhere. I am maybe too judgmental. If I have answered her calls, maybe." He screwed up his brow and turned to her. "But judgment comes, you see. If I make it or somebody else, judgment comes."

She glanced at me. My face had nothing to say to her, so she went ahead. "Mr. Panayotes, we need to ask you a lot more questions. We are going to have to ask you to come with us to the station. Do you understand that?"

He nodded. "Yes, I get my things."

He came very quietly. It was like a different man. He even looked smaller, hunched, with his gaze fixed on the ground as he walked, jutting out his knees. He climbed in the back of the Jag, and Dehan got in beside him. We made it back to Fteley Avenue without uttering a word.

At the station, I explained to Panayotes that he was not under arrest, but that we might hold him for up to seventy-two hours. I told him we'd talk to him in the morning, and meantime I wanted him to think really carefully about what he wanted to tell us about the whores. He listened very carefully, examining my face as I spoke. Then he was led away by a couple of uniforms.

When he was gone, I stepped out into the dusk. The rain had eased for a while, but the breeze was cool and damp. Dehan came after me and leaned on my shoulder.

"I know what you're doing," she said.

"You do?" I looked at her and laughed. "Could you tell me then, because I don't."

"You are thinking—or should I say feeling—that it was too easy. That he is not the guy. That we are being sidetracked by a red herring."

I shook my head. "Not exactly. But we are basing a lot on his personality, on how he talks, and on his weird reaction to Zeta's death."

"He didn't know, Stone. You saw that as clearly as I did. He didn't know whether he'd killed her." She started shaking her head. "No, actually that is not accurate. He was kind of tripping, thinking, 'I didn't kill her, so who did?' It was like he couldn't understand how she got killed if he didn't do it."

"I know."

"He didn't ask how she was killed, where she was killed, when? He didn't ask a single, solitary damned thing. Like he already knew. His only—doubt or uncertainty, I don't know what to call it—was a kind of, 'Uh? But I didn't kill her!'"

"I know."

"So what's troubling you?"

"He's in shock. It is very hard to read the reactions of a person in shock. They can be misleading."

"You're being intuitive and following your feelings. And I know your gut is often right on the money, big guy. But sometimes, just sometimes, you get it wrong."

I smiled at her and raised an eyebrow. "Remind me, I don't recall."

She gazed up at the graying sky. "Well now, my dear Sherlock, there was Sally Jones in 2019, stabbed in her bed while sleeping. Leon Epstein? A million bucks' worth of Mustang?"

"Oh." I nodded. "There was that."

"There were others—"

"A few—"

"And I am telling you, Sensei, this is one of them. Mr. Pany is our guy."

I grunted. "Well, Mrs. Stone, be that as it may, he will keep till tomorrow, and tomorrow he will tell us whatever he has to tell us. Right now, you and I need a damn good rest, a couple of martinis, and a good bottle of wine."

"I am not making moussaka."

"I saved your life. That entitles me to a moussaka."

"Maybe I saved yours."

"We'll do sirloin on the barbeque."

"You got a deal."

SIXTEEN

We stopped at Walgreens and then the Western Beef Supermarket before heading north on White Plaines, taking it easy. We had gotten as far as Morris Park Avenue before either of us spoke. Then I said, "You could have been killed today."

She nodded, keeping her eyes on the road for a while, then turned to look at me.

"So could you. What you did was crazy."

"I was crazy. I was out of my mind. But Dehan?"

She frowned. "What?"

"If I had stayed sane, been responsible..." I trailed off. I couldn't bring myself to articulate the question. I didn't need to. I could see on her face that she had heard it. She looked away. I laughed and said, "I know how badass you are. I know you can take care of yourself, and you're as smart as they come. But none of those qualities would stop him putting a slug through your back."

"I know." She glanced at me and gave a small smile. "I knew you'd come."

Indoors, while I opened the wine and mixed a couple of martinis, Dehan ran upstairs. Then I stepped out to the covered patio, dumped a bag of charcoal into the barbeque, and set fire to it.

I stood a while, listening to the sultry drizzle pattering on the lawn and turning things over in my head. Finally, I grabbed my cell and called Frank.

"I'm about to go home," he said as a greeting, and added, "I have a home. I know because my wife has told me so."

"Hello, Frank. What I have to ask you won't stop you from going home or come between you and your wife."

"I am pretty sure, John, that I have a wife. Otherwise, I have no idea who this woman is who keeps calling to tell me I have a home. How can I help you?"

"I keep turning this question over in my head. How does he know?"

"How does who know what?"

"The Castle Hill Ripper. It has always been assumed, probably correctly, that his hunting ground was Shoprite, and so he probably worked there. But that leaves an important question unanswered. How does he know they are pregnant? None of them was visibly pregnant. They were all in the early stages. So how does he know?"

At the other end of the phone, I heard the car door slam, and his voice, when he answered, was muffled.

"It is a very good question, John, but I am afraid the answer won't help you much. Either he is a gynecologist, which as I recall was a possibility Mike looked into and discarded—"

"Yeah, they had no gynecologist in common."

"Precisely, or, the other possibility is that the killer is sensitive."

"Sensitive? What the hell does that mean?"

"Sensitive, John, in this context means that—" He stopped and sighed. "When women become pregnant, their hormonal balance alters radically because all sorts of processes are required to kick in, in order to feed this foreign body which is now living

COLD BLOOD | 131

inside them. One of the consequences of increased hormonal activity is the discharge of pheromones."

"Slow down a bit, Frank. You hear these terms every day, but I'm not sure I know what a pheromone is as opposed to a hormone."

"In the most basic terms, for the purposes of this conversation, think of them as messengers. Hormones transmit messages within the body; pheromones carry messages outside the body, to other bodies. Now, having said that, Western Man has become so far removed from his natural environment that most people have become completely insensitive to pheromones. Cats, dogs, and wild animals communicate with each other via pheromones very effectively about how they are feeling. But we humans are often completely unaware of how the people around us feel, though we are absorbing their pheromones quite liberally."

I was nodding, watching the coals begin to glow red in the barbeque.

"So you are suggesting that the Ripper might be sensitive to a woman's pheromones and can sense when she is pregnant."

"It's a possibility, yes. And I hate to do this to you, John, but it is worth noting that women tend to be far more sensitive to pheromones than men do."

"Sweet Jesus!"

"Just keep it in mind."

"You think a woman could do this?"

He laughed so loud and so long I had time to drain my martini.

"All I am saying, John," he said, and I could imagine him wiping his eyes with mirth, "is that you should bear in mind that women tend to be more sensitive to pheromones than men. Evolution has designed them that way. But equally, a man who spends a lot of time with women or who grew up in a feminine environment might also develop that sensitivity."

"Okay, thanks, Frank. Enjoy your evening."

"And you yours, John."

He hung up, and I went to pour myself another martini and drop some more ice in Dehan's glass. While I was doing that, she came down the stairs, and I became aware she'd been gone a good ten or fifteen minutes.

"You okay?"

She smiled and nodded. I handed her her glass. She took it and placed it on the breakfast bar.

"I can't," she said.

I frowned. "What?"

She came around into the kitchen and stood in front of me. "I can't have the martini, John."

"What are you talking about?"

She took a step closer and took my collar in her fingers, then took small handfuls of my shirt, staring at my chest. There were tears in her eyes, but a smile teased the corner of her mouth.

"I'm pregnant, Stone."

The room rocked. I felt the kitchen rise up behind me and then swing up behind Dehan. My heart thudded hard, once, high up in my chest. I enfolded her in my arms and bit back hard on the flood of emotion that threatened to overwhelm me. She wrapped her arms around my waist, and we stood like that for a long while. Nightmarish could-have-beens crowded me, trying to force their way into my consciousness. I denied them access, telling myself nothing and no one was going to rob me of this perfect moment. I took a deep breath, smelling her dense, black hair, and asked, "What are we going to call her?"

She pulled back and grinned up at me. "You know it *could* be a boy!"

I emptied the wine and the martini down the sink. "We'll celebrate when he's born," I told her.

We sat outside, listening to the drizzle and drinking soda with ice and lemon, while I seared the steaks over the red-hot charcoal. The flames leapt, licking at the oil on the meat and casting big, dancing shadows against the walls of the house.

"What are you going to do?" I asked her.

"I'm having trouble..." She trailed off, then gave a small laugh. "I was going to say I'm having trouble deciding, but the fact is I'm having trouble even thinking about it. It's been an intense day."

I flipped the steaks, and the flames leapt again, hissing loudly as they consumed the oil and the blood.

"It has that," I said.

"I keep thinking about what you said." I frowned at her, making a question of the frown. "If you hadn't—but then, when you said it, it was if you hadn't come after me. Now—" She gave a nervous laugh. "Now it's if you hadn't come after *us*."

Tears sprang into her eyes, and she put her hand over her mouth. I went and sat next to her and put my arm around her. She stared up into my eyes.

"Stone, there's this tiny"—she showed me what tiny was with her fingers—"there is this tiny person inside me. And I have to protect him or her."

"We both do, Carmen. And we will."

"Stone?"

"Yes."

"The steak is burning, and I really want to eat it." I jumped up to put them onto plates, and as I did so she said, "Do we have mayonnaise? And Branston Pickle?"

NEXT MORNING, we sat in the chief's office. He was watering his bonsai while Dehan and I sat in the two armchairs he had against the wall. Panayotes had been brought up to interrogation room one and was waiting.

Dehan said, "Sir, we have some news."

"Ah." He smiled at the bonsai. "Progress in the case?"

"No sir. I'm pregnant."

He turned and beamed at her. "Do you know, I *thought* so!"

"How?" I asked quickly. "How did you know?"

He shook his head and set down the watering can. "I am sensitive to that kind of thing. There is a look, a glow. I wouldn't know how to explain it. Well, that is extremely good news. Have you thought about what you plan to do? You won't be wanting many more adventures like yesterday's, I presume."

"I only found out yesterday, sir. I need to have it confirmed by the doctor. But I will be staying out of trouble." She gave a small shrug. "Interrogations, desk duties, research."

"Very sensible. Well, there is no hurry. You have some nine months ahead of you in which to meditate about your future options. Keep me posted and, please, do take care."

"And, sir, can we keep this between us until, you know…" She held out her hands in front of her like she was holding a beach ball.

"Of course. It's our secret."

We stepped out of his office and moved toward the interrogation rooms. I stopped her outside the door to number one and asked her, "You sure you're up for this?"

She nodded. "Totally."

I opened the door, and we went in.

Panayotes watched us come in. As I closed the door, he watched Dehan go and sit down opposite him. I went and leaned on the back of my chair.

"What size feet have you got, Hercules?"

He frowned like I had spoken to him in Swahili. "My feet? What size?"

I nodded, and he looked down at his feet, like he had to gauge it. He shrugged, "Forty-one, maybe forty-two."

"That's European size, right? What's that here?"

Dehan said, "You've been here a long time, Panayotes. You must have bought shoes. What size do you buy?"

He seemed to think about it, spread his hands and said, "Nine? Nine and half? Why you want to know size of my feet?"

I pulled out my chair and sat. "You had some time to think."

He nodded. "Who running the store now?"

"Your assistant manager. Hercules, you need to talk to us about the whores and the private deliveries after hours."

"I tell you I am not married. I have to be discreet. I cannot all the time be calling professional women. Too many risks." He put his head on one side, spread his hands. "AIDS, all kinds disease, but also blackmail, and is expensive. If you don't want filthy old bitch, you godda pay." He crooked his index finger and tapped it on the table. "You godda pay good."

Dehan said, "So?"

He looked at me and seemed to appeal for sympathy. "First I am resisting the temptation. But all the time, you know? Women who no got money, no got family, 'Ey, Mr. Pany,' here, 'Ay Mr. Pany,' there, 'Oy Mr. Pany,' here. All the time, 'Bring me some beef I make you special stew from Colombia,' 'Bring me chicken I make you nice chicken from Mexico,' 'Bring me rice and bananas I make special dish from Cuba,' cabbage from Poland, and I am saying, 'No, no, no, no…' until one day I say, 'Okay, I bring to you when I leave the shop. I leave on the step and I ring the bell and I go home to my wife.' She say yes, okay. But when I arrive, she is waiting. 'Come in, come in, have a beer, glass of wine, I make some food, you stay.'" He shrugged elaborately. "What am I? A robot? There is nobody waiting at home. No wife, no kids, no family. So I stay."

I asked, "Who was this woman?"

He stared up at the ceiling. "Maria, Maria, Maria Antonia. She have an apartment on Theriot. Maria Antonia Gutierrez. She tells me she is an architect in Peru. But in America she is cleaner. I say, 'Why don't you stay in Peru, where you are an architect?' She gets mad at me. She is beautiful woman. Now she is teacher at the Pablo Neruda Academy on Lafayette."

I paused to screw up my forehead. "When was this?"

"Christmas 2018. It was nice, but you know, Latina women." He gestured apologetically at Dehan. "No offense, eh? Latina women get mad so easy. So we were okay for Christmas, new year, and I tell her it gotta stop."

Dehan asked, "She didn't get pregnant?"

"No, no, no!" He gave a big, explanatory spread to his hands.

"No! If she get pregnant with my child, I would not leave her." He stretched out those hands, gesturing toward Clason Point. "Is like Zeta. I was crazy mad, telling her is over. But when I think about it"—his face twisted up, and he started to sob—"is my baby. God will punish me. Because I should have forgive her and give her and my baby my home. Instead, I leave them to get killed by that son of a bitch!"

Dehan cleared her throat. "Mr. Panayotes. Will you tell us abut Sandra Gavilan? Did you ever make out of hours deliveries to Sandra?"

"Sandra Gavilan?" He went very still and very quiet. After a moment he said, "Sandra is killed."

She leaned forward and spoke quietly. "Did you take food to her after work?"

He was staring hard at the edge of the table. "I don't remember. Is a long time ago she is killed."

"What about Maria, Mr. Panayotes?"

"Maria? I tell you about Maria."

"Maria Romero, on Olmstead Avenue." Her voice dropped practically to a whisper. "She was pregnant, remember? You thought she was a whore. She called you Pany. Did you take food to her house?"

He shook his head and rubbed his face with his hands. His eyes were staring. "I don't remember."

I said, "Take your time, Hercules. We need to step outside a moment. We'll be right back." I leaned forward. "There was also Angela Garcia, on Underhill Avenue. She was also pregnant. You also thought she was a whore. Think about it. What do you remember?"

I stood, and Dehan followed me out into the corridor. I said, "Either he is a superb actor, or he is having psychotic breaks and truly does not remember the women he killed."

"Or he didn't kill them."

I nodded. "Or he didn't kill them."

She shook her head. "But Stone, it walks like a duck and it

quacks like a duck, but it's a goat? There are too many things that fit. Now it turns out he *has* been making after hours deliveries for *years*! And that long, elaborate story about the girl he started delivering with, *one year after the first killings!* Come on! But ask him about one of the seven, and he goes weird and abstracted and says, 'I don't remember!'"

I studied her face a moment. She looked the color of a church candle.

"You feeling okay?"

"Bit sick."

"You want to go home?" She sagged. "Call a cab. Go home and lie down. You need anything at all, you call me."

"I feel like such a pansy. I should be here, helping."

"You are." I gave her a kiss. "Go call a cab. I'll check on you in half an hour."

I watched her go down the stairs and disappear from view. I stood a while, watching the flow of cops up and down the stairs, and crossing the hall outside the detectives' room at the bottom. I thought about Panayotes, his repeated statement that he did not remember, and his sudden shifts from explosive arrogance to silent introspection.

My cell rang. I looked at the screen and didn't recognize the number.

"Detective John Stone, New York Police Department."

"Detective, this is Oliver Rose, from the Shoprite store."

"Hello, Oliver. What can I do for you?"

"I need to talk to you, sir. As soon as possible."

SEVENTEEN

I pulled up outside Oliver's green clapboard house. The sky was gray, and the road was damp, but there was a break in the clouds. My grandmother used to tell me if the blue in the sky was big enough to fix a sailor's pants, the day would clear. It didn't look to me like it was big enough for that.

I pushed through the gate. A breeze moved the wet leaves on the pin oaks in back, at the end of his lawn. I climbed five steps to his small porch, and the door opened before I could ring the bell. Oliver smiled at me. It wasn't a happy smile. It was the smile you're required to offer a visitor if you're from the Midwest.

"Detective, please come in. Mom has gone to lie down. I wanted to avoid her hearing the bell. She'd feel she had to come down and offer you coffee and apple pie, and I would rather have this conversation in private."

"Sure."

He led me from the small entrance hall to a comfortable living room with a large bow window and an electric heater designed to look like a real fire. There was a sofa and a couple of armchairs arranged around a coffee table, and at the far end, there was a dining table with six chairs in front of a set of French doors. Through them, I could see a paved patio and a waterlogged lawn.

He gestured to a chair and clasped his hands. "Well, my mother isn't with us, but I can offer you coffee, apple pie, or blueberry pie, whatever you prefer."

"I'm fine, thank you, Oliver. I really need to get back to the station house. What is it you wanted to talk about?"

He took a deep breath and sat on the sofa with the gray light of the bow window behind him.

"Detective Stone, I am very conflicted. I was raised strictly Episcopalian, and I was raised to do the right thing. But what do you do when there are two conflicting right things, and both can equally be seen to be the wrong thing?"

I stifled a sigh. "I am not a moral philosopher, Oliver, and I am not especially religious. All I can say to you as a policeman is do what the law requires, and if you have a moral conflict with that, go with the greater good. If you think you might have information that will put an end to the murder of women and their unborn children, then I think your moral obligation is clear."

He closed his eyes and took a deep breath. "Yes, of course you are right. I suppose what I am really hoping for is your reassurance that..." He trailed off, then frowned at the floor. "As I understand it, Detective, reading between the lines, it now seems that David's conviction may be wrong. I just hope that another investigation won't be rushed through and another innocent man won't be convicted on the strength of what I tell you."

I nodded. "All I can tell you, Oliver, is that I am trying to get to the truth of what has happened, and what is happening. I am not going to rush my investigation. On the other hand"—I offered him a tired smile—"if you have information that might be relevant to a homicide investigation, the law requires you to give me that information."

"Of course."

I waited. Finally, he took another deep breath and raised his face to look at me. He still looked unhappy.

"I am not sure if this rates as information. It is more a case of things I have observed over the last three years."

"Let's have it."

"As I have told you, I have a great deal of respect for Mr. Panayotes. A lot of the workers complain about him and say he is rude and aggressive, but I think he operates under a great deal of pressure, and he is basically a fair and honest employer. I have no—"

"Oliver," I interrupted with a smile, "this is what you need to be telling your minister to appease your conscience, but it does not help my investigation. You can skip this bit."

He raised his hands up, like he was making an offering, then dropped them onto his lap. "You're right. Let me start again. You were interested in whether Mr. Panayotes made after hours deliveries to female customers."

"We were, and we still are."

"Of course I don't know what happened in 2018 and 2019 because we were still in North Dakota, but from 2020 to now, I can tell you—" He took another, very deep breath, closed his eyes, and puffed out his cheeks. "I can tell you that he regularly paid visits to *certain* customers."

"Certain customers...?"

"They were always women. It was like a process of—" He shook his head like he was searching for a word and discarding all the wrong ones. "Like a process of serial polygamy."

I raised my eyebrows and smiled. "Serial polygamy?"

"Yes. It has to be said that Mr. Panayotes is apparently very attractive to women. I think it's that noisy, Mediterranean macho thing. A lot of women seem to be attracted to that." He paused and gave his head a tilt to the side. "The truth is he spends at least half of his time in the office. But equally he spends almost half of his time in the store, checking the shelves, checking prices, overseeing the cleaning. He is a very conscientious man. But he *also* spends a lot of that time fooling and joking with the customers. It's great for the shop. They love it. But if you're a little observant you soon notice that he only does that with the women. Sure, he'll joke with the guys, slap them on the shoulder, have a laugh and move on. But with the women, it's different. He will gather several of them around him." He gave a small laugh. "Like a harem, and he will talk to them about prices, about quality, about Greek recipes. He will tease them, joke and, speaking honestly, flirt."

He paused. "Are you sure you won't have a coffee?"

"Quite sure. Tell me about this flirting."

"Well, at first, I thought it was just like a Mediterranean thing. But pretty soon, I began to notice that he would gather a little group and, for a time, a month or six weeks maybe, he would focus on that group. And within that group, he would select one woman and, very subtly, he would focus on *her*. And pretty soon, nine out of ten times, he would start very discretely taking her"—he made quotation marks with his fingers—"'special deliveries.' That would go on for a few weeks, then he would drop that woman and start up a new group."

I frowned and scratched my chin. "Oliver, forgive me saying this, but that is some very acute observation."

He nodded, and his expression was apologetic. "I know, and it's one of several reasons I was reluctant to talk about it. The subject I want to get my degree in, sir, is psychology. It's a subject that fascinates me. It's also the reason I chose this job. It is a perfect place from which to observe people—both customers and employees!"

"Sure, I can see that." I scratched my head. "Tell me something. From your rather special perspective, what did you make of Dave Clark?"

He held my eye a moment and looked acutely embarrassed. "Honestly? Please don't take offense, but it seemed to me to be an absurd arrest, and the conviction astonished me. Sincerely, if it had not been for the confession, I doubt the jury would have convicted. I'd go further and say I doubt the DA would have allowed the prosecution. Dave was just clearly not the guy on so many levels."

"It's interesting that you should say that."

"I mean, going by the very little that was available in the media, the Castle Hill Ripper was a methodical planner with an above average IQ. Dave Clark was frankly chaotic, disorganized, and had an IQ that was well below average. I mean, forgive me if I seem rude, but that case was reflective of the investigating detective's IQ and the jury's IQ. Both were below average."

I laughed, and there was gratitude in his own laugh. "I'm sorry, I don't mean to be rude, but anyone who took the trouble simply to read the papers could see that Dave Clark was not capable of those murders. And, honestly, it left unanswered a question which to me seemed essential—it had to be answered before any conviction could be deemed just."

He paused, watching me, waiting. I said, "How did he know they were pregnant?"

He nodded. "Exactly. How could a man with the IQ of a smart gorilla, with no imagination, with no ability to empathize or put himself in another person's shoes, how could that person know that a woman was pregnant? Especially in the early stages of pregnancy. How would he persuade her to let him into her house?"

I leaned my elbows on my knees and rubbed my face. "So how do those same criteria stack up against Panayotes?"

His face drained of color. "Oh, gosh! I am not saying that I think—"

I raised a hand. "No, I know you're not, Oliver. I'm just interested. You are obviously an observant person, you have several years in the shop, and you have some background in psychology. I am just, off the record, interested in how you, personally, would apply the criteria you applied to Dave, to Panayotes. IQ, empathy..." I trailed off.

He stared at the edge of the coffee table again, rubbing his palm with his left thumb.

"Mr. Panayotes is an intelligent man. You know, anything above one hundred forty-five is genius. I certainly wouldn't put him that high. But he is intelligent, methodical in his thinking, and he has a good feel for people. He reads them well." He paused, gazing out at the gray day. The sailor's pants were gone, and it had started raining again. "But empathy?"

He turned his gaze on me and raised his shoulders an eighth of an inch.

"He is aware of how he impacts other people. He is aware of how people are going to respond to what he says and does. Is that empathy? Is he capable of sympathetic imagination? Can he imagine your pain, your loneliness? I honestly don't know. Sometimes, when he really lays into one of his employees, especially the girls, you might think he has no capacity for empathy at all. But then, perhaps he is just focused on work."

I nodded. "Oliver, this is very helpful. There is one area we have not touched on, and that is the particular women that he established these relationships with. You must realize that there are particular women we are interested in."

"Yes, and that was what made me phone you, Detective. Your colleague, Detective Dehan, said that you were interested in his relationships with his customers. That got me thinking. I googled the names of all the victims of the Castle Hill Ripper and"—he sagged back into his chair—"obviously I can't comment on the first two girls because I was in Drake—in North Dakota—but I can say that the four subsequent girls were among his special friends, ones he delivered to."

"Can you name them?"

"Yes. The first one I was aware of was Nompumelelo Moyo. She was a lovely, warm, beautiful Nigerian woman." He thought for a moment. "Then Caren Mitchell he was with for a month or two, Angela Garcia, a very vivacious, funny woman, and Maria Romero." Something about his manner said he hadn't finished. I waited. Finally, he said, "Last year he seemed to have turned over a new leaf. He kept more to his office, and there was far less of the prancing around the store and gathering women around him. And there were no afterhours deliveries."

"But?"

"But this year, shortly after Christmas, it started again. Just a little to start with, but by Easter, he was in full swing."

"Name?"

"I am sure you have guessed already, Detective. He started making deliveries to Elaine Gallardo. That..." He stared at me for a long moment with his eyes flitting over my face. "That was the real reason he told me not to make any more out of hours deliveries. Because he reserved them for himself." He hunched his shoulders and frowned. "Eh, Oliver, we no makin' deliveries after hours, eh! Is no good for shop's policy!"

I laughed in spite of myself. "That's good. You sound just like him."

He smiled and shook his head. "That man is like Satchmo, or Christopher Walken. So easy to mimic." His face took on a strange rigid look. "You know, Christopher—pause—*Wal*ken, who—pause—emphasizes in all the—*wrong* places." I laughed again, and he shrugged. "My little party piece."

Would you be prepared to make a full statement, with names and dates?"

"Of course. I'll type it up and bring it in tomorrow."

I stared out at the neat lawn with its gray puddles reflecting the gray sky above, thinking of Panayotes sitting waiting for me in the interrogation room. A disembodied voice echoed from above us, and I frowned at Oliver.

"*Ollie! Oliver!*"

He smiled and sighed. "Will you excuse me? My mother has woken up. I'll have to tell her you're here. Do you mind if she comes down to greet you?"

"Of course. That's fine."

He left the room, and I heard his feet tramping up the stairs. I heard his voice. "What is it, Mom? I'm just talking to..." The rest was muffled, lost. I stood and went to the French doors. The row of pin oaks beyond the boggy lawn tossed and nodded gently at me. I thought about Mike and his friendship with Panayotes, I thought about pheromones and how big a part they played in empathy. I thought about Elaine Gallardo peering through her peephole, smiling at the fisheye view of Panayotes' big head, leering and holding up a polystyrene tray of bloody steaks.

"She sends greetings and asks you to forgive her rudeness." I turned as he came through the door. "But she says she is in no condition to receive a guest. She hopes you'll come again soon to try her blueberry pie. She does make a very good blueberry pie. Perhaps you and Detective Dehan. I notice you came alone. I hope she's well. Poor Mom gets so few visitors since we moved here."

I nodded. "Sure. That's very kind. Maybe when we've wrapped the case up. Your dad not around?"

"Oh." He smiled. "He's not part of the picture."

I stepped out into the drizzle. Dusk was closing in. I hunched my shoulders and made my way to the Jag. As I climbed behind the wheel, I pulled out my cell and called Dehan. Her voice was sleepy when she answered.

"Hey, big guy."

"You okay?"

"I'm good. When will you be home?"

"Not long. I'm just wrapping up."

"See you in a bit, then."

"Yeah, see you soon."

But I could tell she was already asleep. I called the chief.

"John."

"Sir, we have a witness who will testify that Hercules Panayotes had intimate personal relationships with five of the victims and made private, afterhours deliveries to their homes."

"That's excellent. Well done."

"But, sir, before we proceed, there is something I need to do. I need the department to fly me to North Dakota. Tomorrow morning."

EIGHTEEN

I touched down at Rugby Municipal Airport in North Dakota the next morning at eleven a.m. Thanks to the exceptional circumstances and the insistence of the chief, the police department had agreed to charter a small plane to take me there. The flight had been slow and painful.

There was a small amount of tarmac, a couple of hangars, and flat green fields as far as the eye could see. The deputy for Drake was there to meet me. He had a red, unmarked Ford pickup that was probably new about the time Eve was selling Adam the line that it was not the Fruit of the Tree of Knowledge, it was just an apple. He was a lean man in his thirties. He sauntered over as I approached and shook my hand like he was testing how solid my arm was.

"Deputy Asher Johnson. People call me Ash."

"Detective John Stone. Thanks for coming to get me."

"You betcha. Sling yer bag in back. Where'd you wanna go?"

I slung my bag in back, climbed in the passenger seat, and slammed the door.

"City Hall, but maybe you can help me along the way."

He turned the key in the ignition. The engine roared, and the chassis rattled violently before settling down into a kind of integrated rumble. It was a stick shift. He rammed it into first to the sound of tortured steel, and we rolled out of the airfield onto the highway and turned south, rising through the gears in a series of painful judders and surges.

"Name it," he said at last. "If I can help, I will."

"Do you remember the Rose family?" He didn't say anything, just kept looking ahead at the road. "They lived on the corner of Main Street and First Avenue."

"I know where they lived."

"So you did know them?"

"We got less than three hundred people in Drake. We all know one'nuther, Detective Stone. What is it you wanna know?"

Something in my head told me less than three hundred people was not a town; it was a clan or a family. So I gave my shoulders a small lift and said, "Mainly a bit of background. Oliver is a resident in my precinct. He's a good kid." I gave Deputy Ash an ironic smile and added, "We could do with a few more like him. He has been very helpful in an investigation we are conducting, but I need to confirm a few details."

He turned to study my face a moment. There was some humor in his eyes, but the rest of his face was like a slab of granite.

"You through with your introduction, Detective?" He looked back at the long, straight road. "The law's the law. You break it, you pay the penalty. That's the way it is. My mom was Oli's mom's cousin. That makes me and Oli some kind of cousins. But if he broke the law, and I am an officer of the law, then I gotta take him down. So now you can ask me."

"Thanks for clarifying that, Ash. The fact is, as far as I am aware, Oliver has not broken any laws. But I do need some details about his background. Like, what happened to his father?"

He straightened and cleared his throat. "Jim Rose wasn't from Drake. He wasn't from the Dakotas. He was from somewhere east. I guess that's why they saddled the boy with a name like Oliver. He wasn't a good man. Talk was that Nora fell crazy for this guy when he drifted into town because he was different." He frowned at me like I'd made a comment he didn't agree with. "In a town of three hundred souls, one hundred fifty is gonna be men. If you're a woman, fifty's gonna be too old, fifty's gonna be too young, which leaves you fifty men you can choose from. Now you gotta remove from them all those men who are closely related to you. If your family's been in Drake for a few generations, you might be lookin' at twenty men, or less, you can hitch up with. Now remove all the guys who's ugly, stupid, drink too much..." He trailed off, shaking his head. "If you's a woman who just wants to settle down and breed, you'll take what's on offer. But Nora wasn't like that. Nora was always a bit more sensitive. She liked to read, listen to classical music, things like that. So when Jim blew in on his Harley, talkin' about ridin' down to California, cultivatin' cannabis in Colorado, playin' in a band I don't know where, well, Nora fell hook, line, and sinker. Pretty soon, they was shacked up and she was pregnant. They never did get married."

"That was Oliver?"

He gave a single downward nod. "He never was baptized, either. His dad was into all that green shit." He glanced at me, like I might be into all that green shit too. "Whole-wheat bread, lentils, and atheism. He drank a lot too. Far as I can tell, he weren't too bothered whether his beer and his whiskey was organic or not. Pretty soon he started beating her. She'd turn up at the store with bruises on her face, black eye, swollen jaw. Peggy'd ask her what happened—"

"Peggy?"

He frowned at me. "At the store."

"Oh."

"She'd ask her what happened. 'Oh, I fell down the stairs,' she'd tell her. I never did see a woman who fell down the stairs so often as Nora Rose."

"How long was he there?"

"Five years all told. One day he beat her so bad it's a miracle he didn't kill her. When he was done, he went down to the bar on the corner. She managed to call the doc, who come round and patched her up. But before he done that, he called my pa. Pete Johnson. Pa was the deputy then like I am now. I must've been fourteen or fifteen at the time. So when Pa saw the state she was in, he calls me, and we went down to the bar together. He says to me, at the door, 'I want you to watch what happens next, Ash.' So we go inside and, real calm and quiet, he tells Jim to step out back with him. Some of his friends made to come too, but he puts his hand on his sidearm and points at them with his other hand, and he says, 'You boys just stay right here and finish your beer.' Then Pa and Jim and me went out back, where the trees are."

He paused a while and nodded a few times.

"Well, everything Jim done to Nora my Pa did to Jim, and then some. He beat that man till he couldn't stand no more. Then he made him stand and hit him again. When he was done, he called the doc, who was still at Nora's place across the road, and says to him, 'Doc, you better come and have a look at Jim Rose. I think he just fell down the stairs.'"

"What happened after that?"

"He puts his hand on my shoulder and points down at Jim. 'That,' he says to me, 'is how you stop a man from beating his wife. Son,' he says. 'I want you to know that I was wrong in what I did. I should have done this a long time ago, and right now Nora wouldn't be in the state she's in.'"

I smiled and thought of Dehan. "I can think of a few people who would agree with him."

"You don't?"

I thought about it for a moment. "I'm a policeman, you're a sheriff's deputy. They are different offices. I am employed by the NYPD, you are deputized by an elected sheriff. I represent the law. You represent the people."

His faint smile said I was talking bullshit. After a moment, he said, "I didn't ask you if the NYPD agreed. I asked you if you agreed. Let me put it to you another way. If it was your mom, your sister, your wife, or your daughter, would you agree?"

I drew breath, but he cut me short.

"Jurisprudence is for men with beards and pipes to sit and talk about in their clubs while they drink fine French cognac. What happens out here—" He pointed at the sparsely spaced houses among the well-tended lawns and the towering oaks and pines. "That's life. When you're looking at a woman with a broken jaw, bloodshot eye, and a broken arm, whose husband is down in the saloon drinking with his buddies, and tonight, tomorrow, the day after, he is gonna come home and do the same again, you can't explain to her about jurisprudence, appointed offices, and elected sheriffs. You need to go and solve her problem."

"Point taken. So after your father had explained to him about respecting his wife, what happened to Jim Rose?"

"He shacked up with one of his pals for a week while he recovered. Then he got in his car, and he left town. We never heard from him again. This is City Hall."

He pulled in beside a small Toyota coupe and pulled on the hand brake with a loud creak. He pointed past me up the road. "Deputy Sheriff's Office is the big white house you can see just there, hundred and fifty yards away, just past the church. That's where you'll find me. Oliver's old house is hundred yards down that way." He pointed in the opposite direction. "The apartment above the hair salon. Anything you need, you let me know."

"Thank you."

I climbed down, grabbed my bag from the back, and watched him drive away. I turned and pushed my way through the glass doors into the small one-story yellow brick building. The door chimed as it opened, and then again as it closed. There was a beige carpet, the walls were paneled in pine, and there were posters about the various ways City Hall could help you to be a better citizen. There was a desk, and behind the desk there was a woman who looked up from her computer screen and smiled at me.

"You must be Detective John Stone, from New York."

I smiled. "Is it that obvious?"

She gave a small, throaty laugh. "Not at all. I just know everybody else. The mayor is expecting you." She pointed past her desk to a set of doors. "Go through there, follow the corridor to the end. It's the last door on your right."

I thanked her and followed her instructions to a plaque that read simply *Mayor Anderson*. I knocked, and the door opened.

He was built like a large oak door. His hair was brilliant white and swept back, and you could have laid foundations with pieces of his jaw. The eyes were sharp and blue, and if you traveled from one shoulder to the other, you'd have to make a stop over at the collarbones.

"Stone? Penny buzzed me. Said you were here. Come on in. You want coffee?"

The office was a good size and functional. It was a place where you worked, not a place where you did politics or pumped your ego. He held out a hand like a tree root, and we shook.

"Thank you, Mayor Anderson—"

"Bill, then I don't have to call you Detective Stone. Sit down."

He leaned over his desk and buzzed. "Penny, let's have a pot of coffee. And see if there are any of Kathy's muffins left."

He went behind his desk, folded himself into his chair, and frowned at me.

"You'll have to explain. The New York Police Department is interested in the Rose family. Oliver Rose left here three years ago. He was planning on doing a degree in psychology. He was a bright kid, did well at school. Why is the NYPD interested in him?" He laughed. "I mean, I assume it's him you are interested in!"

"In a sense, Bill, but I am not looking at any single person. I am looking for background." I hesitated a moment. "I had a talk with Deputy Ash on the way from Rugby, and he told me a little about Jim Rose and how he eventually left town." I smiled. "Apparently he couldn't get on with the stairs in Drake."

He chuckled. It was a comfortable sound. "Ash's dad was probably the best lawman I ever met. Believe me, I have been around. I haven't spent my whole life in Drake. I came back after twenty-five years, having made my fortune, because this town was my family. And Ash's dad made it that way. He drew a line, and you did not cross that line."

"Do you know what happened to Jim Rose?"

He sat and explored his teeth with his tongue for a while. Finally, he said, "John, what I am going to say to you may be no better'n hogwash. There may be no truth in it whatsoever. I want you to know that so you don't come back to me later sayin', Bill, God damn it! You told me—No. This is a very small town. We have less than three hundred inhabitants. That means you get a lot of rumors. But I'll tell you what you don't get, John. You don't get a lot of Chinese whispers. You know what I mean by that?"

I arched an eyebrow. "That the rumors tend to be true?"

It was like he hadn't heard me. "Sam heard Bob telling Frank. Slim's wife heard it from Mrs. Potter and told Penny. That sort of thing. Not Jake told Hal, who told his wife, who told all the girls at the hair salon, who then told their friends at the bingo and Helen then told her husband, who shared it with the barman at the country club. No."

The door opened without a knock, and Penny came in with a tray of coffee and a plate of muffins. She set the tray on the desk, gave a little curtsy, and left. The mayor poured two cups, handed me one, and waved at the muffins.

"Help yourself. They're as good as you'll find anywhere."

As he did just that and bit into it, I said, "So what was the non-Chinese gossip about Jim? I won't hold you to it."

"His drinking pals who looked after him after—" he hesitated, and I put in, "After he fell down the stairs."

"Right, that, they said he had a girlfriend in New York. I don't recall if it was Brooklyn or the Bronx. It was all of fifteen or sixteen years ago, you understand. But apparently, that was what he told them, and that was what was discussed at the bar. He went to New York. Your loss, our gain."

"Right." I broke a muffin in half and bit into it. It was hard to imagine how a muffin could get much better. "So as you say, that was fifteen years ago. How did Oliver and his mother make out for the next fifteen years, till—?"

"That woman." He shook his head. "She worked all the hours that God sent. She cleaned, she cleaned here at City Hall, she worked in the grocery store—you name it, she would do it. And of course, everybody bent over backward to help her and put work her way. And as soon as Oli turned thirteen, he started taking unofficial jobs too, helping out wherever he could. He was a good kid. Took after his mother and her family, thank heavens, rather than after his father."

He peered at me over the rim of his cup with narrowed eyes. "Is this any use to you?"

I took the time to finish a muffin and drain my coffee.

"I don't know yet. I think so."

"You want to tell me what it is you're hoping to find?"

I gave a small laugh. "I want to, but I can't. Partly because it's under investigation, and partly because I am not one hundred percent sure myself."

He refilled my cup, and while he poured, I asked him, "Tell me something. Jim Rose, aside from beating up his wife, was he ever involved in any kind of violence?"

He shook his head as he slid the cup across the desk. "Not that I'm aware of."

"This is a question for the deputy, really, but I'll ask you anyway as I'm here. Thinking back to the time when Jim was here, what about neighboring towns and villages. Were there ever any unsolved crimes of violence against women? In particular pregnant women?"

Now he paused, and his eyes narrowed. "Not that I am aware of, John. But as you say, that is a question for Ash, and more particular for the sheriff in Towner. Rod is a good man, and he'll have all that stuff on file."

I nodded. "The chief has contacted him already. But sometimes there are things that for one reason or another get talked about in the bar, but they don't get reported to the sheriff."

"And ain't that the truth."

"There are just two more things I need from you, Bill. If you can let us have electronic copies of the files relating to Oliver and his mother and Jim, births, deaths, marriages, property held, property sold, all that stuff."

"Of course. Though I have to say I am at a loss as to what you hope to find."

"I know, and also the doctor who attended Mrs. Rose after her last beating, the one that ended their relationship."

He smiled. "Step out of here and cross the road, diagonally to your right. Seth, Dr. Seth Larson."

I stood, thanked him for his hospitality, and left.

NINETEEN

I crossed the road and pushed through the door into the clinic. I was in a waiting room. Four elderly women sat on hardback blue chairs, watching me with unhappy faces. Watching me also was a young woman with platinum hair, very red nails, and pale blue eyes that had never been troubled by curiosity. I gave her a smile for which she had no use and showed her my badge.

"My name is Detective John Stone. I'm with the New York City Police Department, and I'm here by invitation of the sheriff of McHenry County. I'd like to speak with Dr. Seth Larson."

"He's with a patient." She said it with a small side order of attitude.

"I imagine he is, but could you let him know I'm here, please?"

"Even if I let him know you're here, he's still with a patient."

I nodded and put my badge away, then gave a small shrug. "I can let him know myself if it's too much trouble for you." I pointed down a short corridor. "Is it down there?"

"I'll tell him. Sit down. I'll tell you when he's free."

I stood by the door, leaning on the jamb, crossed my arms,

and stared at her. She stared back and picked up a Bakelite telephone that was the latest thing before the Beatles stopped shaving.

"There's a man here who says he's a detective from New York. Says he wants to talk to—" She paused a second, like she'd been interrupted, then said, "A *detective*. Yes, a detective. From New York. Here, yes Dad, here, in the clinic, and he wants to talk to you. I told him—"

She held the receiver in front of her and stared at it. A moment later, a door opened down the corridor, and a slim man in his fifties dressed in a tweed jacket and a spotted bow tie leaned out stared at me, frowning.

"You're a detective from New York?"

"Yes, Doctor. But I can wait—"

"Come in!" He turned and spoke to an invisible woman inside his office. "Take a couple of aspirin, Mrs. Brown, and I'll drop in and see you this evening on my way home. Take a nap. You're probably overtired. With your husband, it's hardly surprising."

Mrs. Brown emerged from the room, paused to stare up into my face, and then left. I entered, and the doctor pointed to the patients' chair at his desk. The desk was littered with papers and files, several medical textbooks, a stethoscope, and a sphygmomanometer. In the corner behind the desk, he had a full-sized human skeleton whose eyes seemed to follow me across the room and who grinned at me as I sat down.

He closed the door and returned to the large, well-used leather chair behind his littered desk.

"Okay," he said, "you have my full attention."

I showed him my badge. "I am here with the knowledge of the county sheriff's office. I have just been speaking to the mayor, and I am hoping you will be able to clarify some points for me."

"About what?"

"About Jim Rose."

He made a big, silent O with his mouth and nodded several

times before saying, "Of course, New York. He went to New York, didn't he?"

"I don't know. According to the mayor, that is a rumor devoid of Chinese whispers."

He snorted a laugh. "That sounds like Bill. What he means is it is only a rumor, but you can be damned sure it's true. However, now I am more mystified than before. If you don't know that Jim Rose is in New York, why the hell are you looking for information about him all the way out here?"

"What I really need, Doctor, is to understand two things. The first is what kind of relationship Jim Rose had with his son, Oliver. I understand you're not a psychologist, but I am not looking for a psychologist's diagnosis either. What I need at this stage is an informed, intelligent medical view on their relationship. You won't be called on to testify."

He watched me carefully until I had finished and then grunted. "And the second thing?"

"I'd like you to tell me, in as much detail as you can, exactly what happened the night Jim beat his wife for the last time, before Deputy Johnson—"

"This deputy's father, Pete, yes. Before he took matters into his own hands."

"Right."

He slumped back in his chair and swiveled it slightly so he could look at the wall, like he had his thoughts spread out there for examination. He seemed to look them over for a moment and then sighed.

"Taking your questions in order, as far as Jim's relationship with his son is concerned, I'd have to say it barely existed. Oliver was raised by his mother. She cared for him, educated him, fed him, dressed him, everything. Once Jim had gone, she returned to the church, and of course the town rallied around her and helped in any way we could. I suppose Oliver must have been four or five years old. He did well at school, he was bright, had a charming personality, much like his mother, and as soon as he was old enough, he started taking jobs so he could help her financially. But his relationship with his father was nill."

"What about his relationships with other people in the town, friends...?"

"He formed friendships in the normal way. He had a couple of girlfriends, hung out with a few pals." He was frowning. "Why do you ask?"

"I am trying to get a picture, Doctor."

"Of *what?*"

"If you could tell me about what happened that night, I will have a better idea."

Irritation flickered in his eyes. He took a deep breath and spread his hands. "It was nothing new. He used to beat her regularly. She would often come to me with bruises that had clearly been caused by abuse, but she refused to bring charges, as is so often the case with beaten women.

"They had been together I suppose about five years. Oliver was about five, so perhaps it was a little more. What was new was that this time she called me. I received a telephone call from her late in the afternoon. I remember it vividly. Her voice..." He trailed off and shook his head. "She sounded as if she was going."

I frowned. "Going?"

"Slipping away, dying. She was barely audible. All she could do was repeat the word 'help.' Fortunately, I recognized her voice, otherwise I wouldn't have known where to go. I grabbed my bag and I ran. It's about a hundred yards down the road. The street door and the door to the apartment were both open. I ran up the stairs and found her lying on the floor."

"In which room?"

He stared at me, with his eyebrows raised. "In which room? Is that relevant?"

"It might be."

"She was in the living room, lying on the floor. As I say, it was a miracle he hadn't killed her. The blood..." He trailed off again.

"Blood? From a beating?" He nodded. "Did he use a weapon? Where was the blood from?"

"From her miscarriage. She was hemorrhaging. He didn't use a weapon. It seems she told him she'd become pregnant again. It sent him into a rage. He told her they couldn't afford another child. It was bad enough having to feed one. How were they going to cope with two? They argued, and he started to beat her. First in her face, and then punching and kicking her in her belly, with the deliberate intention of causing a miscarriage.

"I did what I could for her, but before I cleaned her up, I called Pete—Deputy Johnson—so he could see with his own eyes what that bastard had done." He sat in silence for a moment, then added, "May God forgive me. After he'd left, I cleaned her up and got her into bed, and about twenty minutes later, he called me from the bar and told me Jim had fallen down some stairs, could I patch him up."

"Where was Oliver during all this?"

"That poor child was right there, sitting on the sofa in the most absolute silence. His face was like a sheet of paper. White! He didn't cry. He was probably in a state of shock. He just sat there and stared at his mother."

"Doctor, do you happen to know if Jim was a hunter?"

"You do ask some peculiar questions, Detective Stone. In fact, now that you mention it, he was not a hunter when he arrived, but he took to it. His friends were hunters, and he used to go with them. Having said that, everybody hunts around here. I don't because I am a vegetarian, but pretty much all the men, and the boys for that matter, they all hunt."

I made to stand. "Doctor, I won't take up any more of your time. You've been very helpful."

He held out a hand, palm down, to stop me.

"Now hang on just one second, Detective. Is Oliver in any kind of trouble? We do worry about him sometimes, you know. You couldn't find a kinder, more humane boy. But he is—" He paused to search for the word. "He is a little naïve and *sensitive*."

"Sensitive?"

"Yes, he takes after his mother in that. Certainly not his father."

"No, he's not in any kind of trouble. He is a good kid. I know he's doing his best to adapt. The Bronx is a very different place from here, as I'm sure you can imagine. But he seems to be holding it together. He's cheerful, his house is clean and well-kept, and he holds down a job while he's studying and looking after his mother..."

I trailed off because the doctor's face had changed. He'd narrowed his eyes at me like I was talking word soup of a sudden.

"He does *what?* His *mother?*"

"Yes, they moved down together in 2020. Surely you knew that?"

"His mother *died* at the end of 2019. He had been trying to persuade her to move to New York after he tracked down and visited his father the year before. She refused adamantly. But her health was fragile. She never really recovered from the beating." He paused, studying my face. "We have very severe winters and summers here, Detective. And in 2019, she died of pneumonia. That's why Oliver was able to sell up and move to New York."

"You are telling me Nora Rose, Oliver Rose's mother, is dead?"

"Of course! I can show you her death certificate. I signed it myself."

"And he was in New York in 2018."

"Yes, for the whole year. He stayed with his father."

"Sweet Jesus!" I pulled my cell from my pocket and called the chief.

"John—"

"Sir, we need to dispatch a team to pull in Oliver Rose, immediately!" I gave him the address. "Tell them to proceed with extreme caution, he could be very dangerous. And sir—"

"Yes, John."

"Send a car to my house. I want an armed cop with Dehan. He might already have chosen his next victim."

"Dear God! Are you serious?"

"I'm on my way back."

I stood, and as I did, I called Dehan. She answered with her mouth full.

"Humph,"

"Dehan, listen to me. Do not open the door to anybody. Wear your sidearm at all times, and keep the house locked until I get back. Do you understand?"

"Of course not. What are you talking about?"

"Oliver is our guy, and there is a chance he may have realized you're pregnant. If he comes to the house, do not open the door to him."

"*Oliver?*"

"Yes. He was in New York in 2018 and returned to Drake 2019, which was when his mother died."

"Holy…"

"Stay in the house. The chief is sending a car. Let me know when it arrives."

I ran with the doc yelling after me. As I ran, I called Deputy Ash.

"Sheriff's office."

"Ash, this is Stone. I need a ride back to Rugby and a flight back to New York, immediately."

"Guy who brought you is probably still refueling. Where are you?"

"Arriving at your office."

It is about one thousand four hundred miles from Rugby, North Dakota to New York, and by the time we got back to the airfield, filed the flight plan, checked and refueled the plane, and taken off, it was closing on three p.m. The flight was unendurable.

Some stupid voice in my head told me that if I slept, the time would pass faster, but my mind was racing, and sleep was not an option. And as I stared down at the vast, sweeping landscapes below, it seemed to me that they crawled by so slowly they were virtually immobile.

Afternoon turned to late afternoon, which in turn became dusk, where the sky ahead of us turned briefly to blood red and then drained into evening. By the time we touched down at Teterboro in New Jersey, it was eight o'clock, and I felt nauseous.

I climbed in the Jag in the parking lot and called Dehan. The phone rang several times, then went to voicemail. I pulled out of the airport and headed toward Manhattan.

"Hey, Siri, call the chief."

It rang twice.

"John, where are you?"

"Driving into Manhattan. Did you pick up Oliver Rose?"

"I have an unmarked car sitting outside his house. There is nobody home."

"You have someone with Dehan?"

"There's a car outside your front door and an officer inside the house with her."

"Okay. I'm going to check on her, and I'll report tomorrow."

"You're sure Oliver is our man? I don't doubt you, John. But it seems hard to believe."

"I'm sure of it, sir."

"Very well, I'll wait for your report tomorrow."

I hung up and tried Dehan again. Again it went to voicemail. I felt sick but told myself I was worrying unnecessarily. She was probably just resting. There was a patrol car outside and an armed officer inside, and Dehan was well able to look after herself.

I sent her a WhatsApp voice message.

"Hey, I'm trying to call you. Let me know when you're awake."

I saw the two ticks appear in gray as the message was delivered.

Then I saw them turn blue as the message showed as viewed and then heard. I smiled, relief momentarily easing the burn in my belly. I waited for the call, but it didn't come.

"Hey, Siri, call Dehan."

It rang and rang—and went to voicemail.

TWENTY

I pulled up outside my house. The patrol car was there, blocking the entrance. Inside the house, the lights were on. I got out and crossed to the car. Sergeant Sanchez lowered the window.

"Good evening, Detective."

"Evening. Nobody's gone in or out?"

"Only Gillespie. She's watching TV, and Detective Dehan is upstairs lying down."

"No other activity?"

"Not a thing."

"Great."

I moved toward the house, and he called after me, "By the way, I thought you'd like to know, Gordon's been in for surgery. She's in the clear."

I smiled. "Thanks, Sanchez. I'll go see her in the morning."

I approached the house, climbed the steps, and opened the door with my key, calling out as I did so, "Officer Gillespie? It's Detective Stone. Dehan? It's me!"

I moved into the living room. The TV was on. The reason Gillespie had not answered me was because her throat had been cut. The room rocked violently. For a moment, violent, insane terror raced through me. My belly burned hot, and my heart pounded high up in my chest.

Then I was possessed by a cold logic, a knowledge that if Dehan still lived, her survival depended on my freezing my emotions. The rage, the terror, the grief, they could all be expressed later. Right now, I had to be ice.

I took in the copious blood that had drenched Gillespie's uniform, the armchair, and the carpet. I could not call Sanchez and his partner. If Dehan was still alive, calling them could cost her her life. There were no bloody footprints. He had stood behind her, probably come in through the kitchen.

I crossed the room and climbed the stairs.

"I'm in the bedroom." It was Dehan's voice. "I've been waiting for you."

For a moment, it seemed reality itself was disintegrating. The blood seemed to be draining from my face and even my brain. I stepped forward and pushed open the bedroom door.

She was on the bed. Her wrists were cuffed to the bedstead, and her ankles were tied to the foot. She had a gag in her mouth, but her eyes were closed. There was no blood anywhere.

He was sitting beside the bed, watching me, laughing. The bed was between us, and in his right hand he had a long, slim blade. It was bright and looked razor sharp. He had raised her shirt as far as her ribcage, and the blade was resting on her naked belly.

"I'm evolving," he said. He was smiling. "She's in no pain at the moment. Benzodiazepine. It will hurt, of course, when I cut her open. That will wake her up—briefly."

"I had begun to think it might have been your father. But it was you."

"Intelligence is inherited from the mother's side most often. My father was a very stupid, brutish man. I inherited my mother's intelligence and subtlety and my father's appetite for blood."

"You don't need to do this."

There was a touch of reluctance in his smile now. "In fact,

Detective, what you just said is a cliché, and I do, actually, *need* to do it." He tapped Dehan's belly a couple of times with the blade and traced it along under her navel, watching my face. "I tried. After Dave was arrested and convicted, I thought maybe I had satiated myself, but by the end of the year, I was craving. I *needed* that feeling. In fact, so far from being satiated, the need is getting stronger, and it may be your fault." He tapped the blade on her belly again, and his eyes lit up. "Now, how would *that* feel?"

"There are two cops outside. I am here, and I am armed. There is a BOLO out for you. You killed Gillespie downstairs. You can't possibly hope to escape."

He raised the knife and waved it at me. "Hopelessness is a powerful motivator. Nothing left to lose. Besides, has it occurred to you that there may be an unconscious drive in me, seeking to be punished?"

"Then give yourself up."

"Simplistic, Detective Stone. You can do better than that. I was quite content. I had my two orgies a year, the cops were completely fooled, that jackass Dave was where he belonged, in prison, and I had Mr. Pany all lined up to replace him. It was sweet. And then you came along with your exquisite partner." He closed his eyes and took a deep breath through his nose. "Mmm-mmm, just *stinking* of pheromones." He laughed. "I thought I was good for the next six months, but when I smelled Detective Dehan, that urge was there again, hungry for her blood. And then to make matters worse, Pany's little bitch gets torn apart by some animal copycat. How much can a boy tolerate, Detective Stone? And who better to take me in and punish me than big old daddy-to-be Stone? It was too good."

"You came to visit your dad in 2018. You were already feeling the drive back then."

He smiled. "You want to keep me talking in the hope you'll get a chance to shoot me? Who knows, maybe we'll both get lucky. Yes, Detective Daddy Stone, I was feeling the urge, but you can't really go on a killing spree in a village of three hundred people. So I traced my father and went to visit and guilt trip the alcoholic wreck. While I was there, I found myself a job in the rich pastures of Shoprite. Had a superb year and then went back to Drake to try to convince Mom to sell up and move to the Big Apple."

"She refused, so you killed her. But her voice. I heard her call you at your house."

"A recording. Of me. As you know, I am a superb mimic. I keep her presence around the house. We chat often. Didn't you see her at the window? I didn't *kill* her exactly. It was a cold November. A few more blankets might have kept her going another month, but she was on her way out. I just helped her along. Now she's with that God who helped her so much during her lifetime."

"Your gift for mimicry. That's how you killed Elaine Gallardo. You delivered the things she'd left behind—"

"That *I kept* behind, Daddy Stone. Don't underestimate my skills. She was in a flap, filling her bags, and I slipped a couple of things aside. She never noticed till it was too late."

"You are so"—I forced a laugh—"pleasantly Midwestern, yes ma'am, no ma'am, I brought your groceries, ma'am. No one ever perceived you as a threat. You were exactly the profile we drew up, and that's exactly why we didn't notice you." I pointed at his feet. "You're even a size nine. She let you in, you killed her, had your shower, and when you left you took her phone. It was missing from the apartment. Next day, Sunday, at work, you probably went to the bathroom and called Panayotes, mimicked her voice, and asked him to thank you for delivering the groceries. Placing her as alive long after you had been to her apartment. Then what? You returned, put the eggs on to boil, set the timer, and left."

He raised the knife again and wagged it at me. A sixth sense, some kind of intuition told me that the next time he did it, when he brought the blade down, he would kill her. He said, "Cold, calm, and methodical. That is the secret. Like the hunt. Work it out, have a plan, execute it calmly, and bag the prize."

"That's your father, not you."

"Ha! In his dreams! Do you think that simian drunk could have manipulated Dave Clark the way I did? I spent months working on him until in the end he didn't know himself whether he was the Castle Hill Ripper. I *fed him false memories, for Christ's sake!* Could old Pop have done that?"

"Do you remember?"

"Is this the part where we have to endure the amateur psychology?"

"You remember what he did to your mother?"

His voice became shrill. "I will never *forget*. I sat there transfixed as he beat her. He was all power, and she was all stupidity and weakness. I watched her collapse, all the blood pouring out everywhere. Everywhere I looked, there was the blood he had let from her belly. She was useless! A useless lump of meat. But he—*he*—he strode from that room like a giant. He, he went to get a *beer!*" He laughed out loud. "That is superiority! That is power. He destroyed two lives with his bare hands and then strode out to get a *beer!* That is power!"

"You think so? He didn't look so powerful by the time Deputy Pete Johnson had finished with him, did he?"

"Because he was stupid. If he had had intelligence—"

I cut across him. "He was a loser, Oliver. And you inherited your mother's intelligence, but you know what? She was a loser too. And you? You are inhabited and controlled and possessed by two damn *losers!*"

He did it again. He raised the knife and pointed it at me. He was saying something, but I wasn't listening, because I knew that on its return journey that knife was going to plunge into Dehan's belly. He was screaming, a horrible sound like a crazed parrot, "*I am not a loser!*" And I could see in slow motion the long, thin razor-sharp blade moving by fractional degrees, switching its position in his hand.

My own hand was moving. I had absolute certainty that I

could not fumble. There could be no snag, no hesitation, no doubt.

The needle-like blade was no longer pointing at me. It now protruded from the lower part of his fist, pointing down at her tender lower abdomen. His face was twisted with grotesque rage, flushed red, spittle flying from his mouth as he screeched an inarticulate noise. The Sig was in my hand. Moving too slowly. The tip of the blade was an inch from her skin. The Sig moved an inch in a fraction of a second, and the world exploded.

The slug tore through his throat, ripped out three of his vertebrae, and killed any messages traveling from his brain to his hand. The second slug hit the center of his forehead and exploded from the back of his head. He fell backward, taking down the chair and the bedside table as he went.

I stood frozen, trembling. I heard car doors slam, tramping feet, breaking glass, and voices. Somebody swore. Somehow, I managed to shout, "*Upstairs! Clear!*"

And then the feet were running. They came in, training their weapons on me. Gillespie had been alive when they had last seen her. As far as they knew, nobody had entered the house but me. I pointed at Oliver on the floor beside the bed.

"He must have come in through the kitchen. Uncuff her. Call the chief," I said. "Call it in."

They removed her cuffs. I got on my knees beside her, removed the gag from her mouth, and took her hand in both of mine. And then I wept as I hadn't wept since I was a child.

EPILOGUE

THERE WAS A GLOW TO HER SKIN AND A BRIGHTNESS TO her eyes. There was an Atlantic, New England bluster coming in off the sea, riding the small breakers on Hunnewell Beach. We walked in silence, barefoot in the surf, carrying our shoes slung around our necks. She came and clung to my arm with the wind whipping her hair across her face.

"Did I tell you?" she said.

"Probably not. What?"

"We're going to have a baby."

"No kidding!"

"Doc asked if I wanted to know whether it was a boy or a girl."

"What did you say?"

"I said I didn't want to know."

"Good."

"I'm thinking about lunch."

"It's eleven a.m., and you are craving salmon, oranges, mayonnaise, and Branston Pickle."

She nodded, and we began to cross the sand, moving toward the car.

"I went to get coffee," she said.

It had been like that for a few weeks. She would suddenly return to that day. Bring out one single memory and examine it. I would listen and try to ignore the anxiety and the fear it brought back to me.

"He was just there. In the kitchen. Smiling at me. You told me to have my sidearm. I reached for it, but he was so fast. He had the needle in my arm, and all I could see was his face, grinning."

I put my arm around her shoulder, and she put both her arms around my waist.

"He must have lowered me to the floor. Gillespie was watching TV and didn't hear anything. Poor Gillespie." Then she looked up into my face. "Poor you."

I smiled to hide the pain and the fear I still felt. "Poor me? Right now, I am the luckiest man on the planet."

A little later, we were at The Spinney eating oysters and looking out at the sea, sipping iced tea.

"It shook me," I said. "More than I can express."

She watched me. After a moment, she said, "I know. I can imagine."

"I was powerless. And you were slipping away."

"But we are here, now, all three of us."

"I want to keep it that way, Dehan. I'm going to take early retirement."

She smiled. "Good. But won't that drive you crazy?"

"No, because I am going to write my memoirs."

"Your memoirs? This I must read!"

"These. There will be lots of them. I thought I'd start when we were given the cold cases, and you became so obviously infatuated with me."

"Oh, I remember it well."

"I'll use a pseudonym, obviously. Ambrose Armitage or Chase Cavendish—"

"Something a bit more butch, maybe Dan Denver."

"Something like that, but it has to be alliterative. I started writing this morning, while you were sleeping."

"Really?"

I reached in my pocket and pulled out a notebook, turning to the first page.

"You remember Captain Cuevas?"

"Will I ever forget her? She brought us together."

"I thought something like this, a bit *noir*, you know? Dashiell Hammett, Chandler—"

"I like it."

I cleared my throat. "It goes like this: 'The door was open, but I knocked anyway. The captain looked up from her desk. She was one of those women who should have been attractive. She had thick black hair and deep brown eyes, and olive skin that in her mid-forties looked like it was still in its twenties. She had all the right bits in all the right places, but she was somehow unlovable…'"

Don't miss CURTAIN CALL. The riveting sequel in the Dead Cold Mystery series.

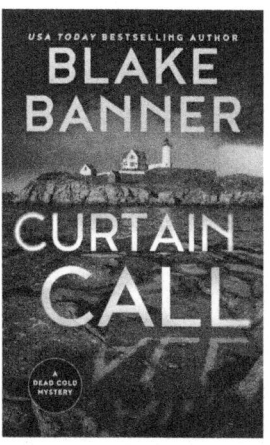

Scan the QR code below to purchase CURTAIN CALL.

Or go to: righthouse.com/curtain-call

NOTE: flip to the very end to read an exclusive sneak peak...

DON'T MISS ANYTHING!

If you want to stay up to date on all new releases in this series, with this author, or with any of our new deals, you can do so by joining our newsletters below.

In addition, you will immediately gain access to our entire *Right House VIP Library*, which includes many riveting Mystery and Thriller novels for your enjoyment!

righthouse.com/email

(Easy to unsubscribe. No spam. Ever.)

ALSO BY BLAKE BANNER

Up to date books can be found at:
www.righthouse.com/blake-banner

ROGUE THRILLERS
Gates of Hell (Book 1)
Hell's Fury (Book 2)

ALEX MASON THRILLERS
Odin (Book 1)
Ice Cold Spy (Book 2)
Mason's Law (Book 3)
Assets and Liabilities (Book 4)
Russian Roulette (Book 5)
Executive Order (Book 6)
Dead Man Talking (Book 7)
All The King's Men (Book 8)
Flashpoint (Book 9)
Brotherhood of the Goat (Book 10)
Dead Hot (Book 11)
Blood on Megiddo (Book 12)
Son of Hell (Book 13)

HARRY BAUER THRILLER SERIES
Dead of Night (Book 1)
Dying Breath (Book 2)
The Einstaat Brief (Book 3)
Quantum Kill (Book 4)
Immortal Hate (Book 5)
The Silent Blade (Book 6)
LA: Wild Justice (Book 7)

Breath of Hell (Book 8)
Invisible Evil (Book 9)
The Shadow of Ukupacha (Book 10)
Sweet Razor Cut (Book 11)
Blood of the Innocent (Book 12)
Blood on Balthazar (Book 13)
Simple Kill (Book 14)
Riding The Devil (Book 15)
The Unavenged (Book 16)
The Devil's Vengeance (Book 17)
Bloody Retribution (Book 18)
Rogue Kill (Book 19)
Blood for Blood (Book 20)

DEAD COLD MYSTERY SERIES
An Ace and a Pair (Book 1)
Two Bare Arms (Book 2)
Garden of the Damned (Book 3)
Let Us Prey (Book 4)
The Sins of the Father (Book 5)
Strange and Sinister Path (Book 6)
The Heart to Kill (Book 7)
Unnatural Murder (Book 8)
Fire from Heaven (Book 9)
To Kill Upon A Kiss (Book 10)
Murder Most Scottish (Book 11)
The Butcher of Whitechapel (Book 12)
Little Dead Riding Hood (Book 13)
Trick or Treat (Book 14)
Blood Into Wine (Book 15)
Jack In The Box (Book 16)
The Fall Moon (Book 17)
Blood In Babylon (Book 18)
Death In Dexter (Book 19)
Mustang Sally (Book 20)

A Christmas Killing (Book 21)
Mommy's Little Killer (Book 22)
Bleed Out (Book 23)
Dead and Buried (Book 24)
In Hot Blood (Book 25)
Fallen Angels (Book 26)
Knife Edge (Book 27)
Along Came A Spider (Book 28)
Cold Blood (Book 29)
Curtain Call (Book 30)

THE OMEGA SERIES
Dawn of the Hunter (Book 1)
Double Edged Blade (Book 2)
The Storm (Book 3)
The Hand of War (Book 4)
A Harvest of Blood (Book 5)
To Rule in Hell (Book 6)
Kill: One (Book 7)
Powder Burn (Book 8)
Kill: Two (Book 9)
Unleashed (Book 10)
The Omicron Kill (Book 11)
9mm Justice (Book 12)
Kill: Four (Book 13)
Death In Freedom (Book 14)
Endgame (Book 15)

ABOUT US

Right House is an independent publisher created by authors for readers. We specialize in Action, Thriller, Mystery, and Crime novels.

If you enjoyed this novel, then there is a good chance you will like what else we have to offer! Please stay up to date by using any of the links below.

Join our mailing lists to stay up to date -->
righthouse.com/email
Visit our website --> righthouse.com
Contact us --> contact@righthouse.com

 facebook.com/righthousebooks
 x.com/righthousebooks
 instagram.com/righthousebooks

EXCLUSIVE SNEAK PEAK OF...

CURTAIN CALL

CHAPTER 1

"You know *Murder She Wrote* was filmed in California, right?"

I said it as I read through the details of a four-bedroom house in Rye, New Hampshire. This one was only a million and a quarter bucks. She didn't answer. I sipped cold coffee from my cup and glanced at where she was sitting at the breakfast table staring at the screen of her laptop. The morning sunlight lay gentle across her face.

"Do we need four bedrooms?" I asked.

She didn't look at me, but she said, "Mm-hmm."

My gaze dropped to her belly. You couldn't see the bulge yet. "Needs a little brother or sister, right?"

"Mm-hmm." This time she said it in more of a rising singsong.

"If we sell your apartment and my house and the Jag, we can raise a little more than half of what we need."

"We're not selling the Jag, Stone."

"I could probably raise..."

"Nope."

"...fifty or sixty grand..."

"Nope."

"...on the open market."

"Nope." She flopped back in her chair, sighed, and rubbed her face. "It has to be near the sea, the Atlantic, it must have white sand and cliffs, and very green countryside. It's got to be clapboard and have a gabled roof and four bedrooms: one for us, one for each kid, and one for guests who come to visit."

"I am with you on every detail. I just need you to tell me how we raise one and a quarter million bucks without saddling ourselves with a prohibitive mortgage. We are both giving up work, remember?"

She didn't get to answer because my phone rang. The screen said it was the chief. It was my day off, and I thought about not answering.

"Sir, good morning."

"John, I am sorry to disturb you on your day off. It's uh..." He hesitated for a moment. "It's a little odd. Somebody has called me and asked specifically to talk to you. She says she is an old friend."

I frowned. "Oh, what's her name?"

I put it on speaker and laid it on the table. He was still hesitating.

"In fact, she said she was an old *flame*."

I saw Dehan's eyebrows rise. My frown deepened. "What's her name, sir?"

"Jane Morley, the actress."

Dehan leaned back in her chair with her eyebrows all the way up. "Jane Morley is an old flame of yours? You had a thing with *Jane Morley?*"

My frown turned into a wince, and I shook my head. "It was very brief. Sir, did she say what it was about?"

"Yes. It's a cold case. It must be a few years ago now. Her personal assistant was murdered, here in the Bronx, in very odd circumstances. But there was a complete dearth of evidence, and the case went cold."

"I remember."

"You were offered the case, and you refused to take it because you'd had a personal involvement with Ms. Morley."

Dehan was shaking her head. I covered the mouthpiece and said, "It was shortly before we met."

The chief said, "She says she has new evidence, but she will only speak to you. You don't have to take it if you don't want to, John. You can very legitimately—"

Dehan cut across him with her high eyebrows again. "Is there any reason why you wouldn't take it, Stone?"

"No." I said it with a little more firmness than was absolutely necessary. "Have her come in tomorrow morning, and we'll hear the new evidence—if there is any."

He said he'd arrange it, and we hung up.

"How come you never told me?"

I shrugged. "There was nothing to tell. It was a couple of weeks, maybe a month, and frankly, I had forgotten. Are you mad?"

"No, I'm not mad. But it's hard to believe you had an affair with one of America's sweethearts and you didn't remember." She frowned. "Haven't she and Danny Santos been married for about twenty years? Stone, did you have an affair with a married woman?"

I sighed. Before I could answer, she was talking again. "Is *that* why you never told me? Mr. Do-It-Right Rectitude had an affair with a married woman? Not *just* a married woman, your honor, but America's Sweetheart Jane Morley!"

"Are you going to shut up any time soon?"

"I am not sure. Depends what you're going to tell me."

"She was the friend of a friend of a friend, and we met at a barbeque given by the friend. We got on well. She was funny and a bit naughty, and I guess I was in the market for a bit of that." I shrugged. "She told me her marriage to Danny Santos was a marriage of convenience arranged by their agents and the studio and that it was open, as long as they were very discreet."

"A marriage of convenience?"

"Yeah. The way she described it to me was that it was like an extension of their movies and the TV show. The fans wanted it, the studio provided it, and she and Danny got paid handsomely for it."

"Huh, so how did it end?"

"Quickly. We had fun, but I was aware it wasn't going anywhere, and she told me she had met a guy who was going to be really useful in her career, and was I the jealous type?"

"And you said you weren't." She smiled.

"Pregnancy has clearly affected your memory, kiddo. I told her I wasn't *French*, and though it had been fun, it wasn't my scene. And that was how we left it."

She nodded a bit, like she was weighing up the data. "And the murder?"

I stood and carried my cup to the table. She had the coffee pot there. I refilled us both and sat.

"This would have been about ten years ago. She had a personal assistant"—I paused to think for a moment—"Katy Hagan. She'd been with her for years. I'd met her briefly in passing a couple of times. She was very efficient, and Jane depended on her totally."

"Did she know you were having an affair with Jane?"

I smiled at her. She was already on the case. "I guess so. Obviously we didn't discuss it, but I assumed at the time that she did. She knew everything about Jane."

I took a sip of brew, allowing my mind to move back and uncover the events at the time.

"I guess it was a few months after we stopped seeing each other. Katy's body was found in a room at the Seven Nights Hotel on Bruckner Boulevard down by Westchester Creek."

"What the hell was she doing there?"

I nodded. "That was one of the questions they were asking back then. Benini had the case, and he asked me if I had any idea. I didn't. I hardly knew the woman, and I knew nothing about her private life. I can only imagine that she was meeting someone, and either that person killed her or it was opportunistic."

She turned in her chair and stretched out her legs, crossing her boots at her ankles.

"What about the killing?"

I stared at her face a moment, remembering, nodding softly. "Brutal," I said. "The lab said there was very little forensic evidence, but what they could say was that it was a powerful guy. Strong, he beat her up badly, broke several bones, then stabbed her several times with a knife."

"Sounds like a crime of rage."

I screwed up my face and made a "Nyeah" sound. "Yeah, it sounded that way to me at the time and certainly has those features. But maybe *not* because on the one hand, they could find nothing in the hotel room that tied the killer to her, and nobody they spoke to who knew her could think of anyone in her life that was that physically powerful and that intensely involved with her." She grunted, and I added, "Also—and this was a contributing factor to my pulling out of the relationship—show biz people live in each other's pockets. There is no such thing as a private life. They just don't understand the concept. So from what Benini told us, everyone from Jane down to the props manager and the lighting assistant knew everything about Kate's private life, and what they knew was that she didn't have one because Jane and Danny had her going non-stop twenty-four seven."

She screwed up her brow. "Wait, there is something wrong here." I nodded, but she ignored me and went on. "If Danny and Jane had her going non-stop twenty-four seven, that explains why she had no private life, but it raises a big mother of a question mark over what the hell she was doing at that hotel."

"Agreed."

"The next logical deductive step is that she was there for one of them."

"The next logical deductive step? Where is the wild, foul-mouthed Bronx urchin I fell in love with?"

"Shut up. Is Danny Santos big and powerful? He looks regular sized on screen."

"I never met him."

She smiled and winked. "Looks like you are going to now."

I shrugged. "If we take the case."

"Oh, we gonna take the case, blanquito." She said it with heavy Latino overtones, shifting her head from side to side. "You *know* we gonna take the case."

DEHAN and I entered Interrogation Room Three with three paper cups of qua-coffee, or what my aunt used to call gnat's pee. As Dehan put the cups on the table, Jane stood and came around the table to take hold of my hands and gaze up into my eyes. At forty, she was still very attractive without the help of surgery.

"John." She said it like it was a whole sentence, with meaning and everything.

I gave her my blandest smile. "Hello, Jane. This is Detective Carmen Dehan, my partner. I was very sorry to hear about Kate." I gestured to her chair. "Won't you sit down?" She backed away a couple of steps, glanced at Dehan, glanced back at me, and sat.

"I was asked to take the case," I told her, "but because we had had a recent personal connection, I refused. Now I understand you have fresh evidence."

She stared at me for a long moment, then looked at Dehan again. "He always was like this. We only dated for about a month, but even back then, he was Mr. Right-and-Proper. It was refreshing for a while, compared with the narcissistic moral cripples I usually date. But you know, I do like a hug and a kiss sometimes and 'Jane, you're as beautiful as ever'—is that too much to ask for?"

Dehan didn't so much chuckle as chortle. Jane turned to me

and pointed at Dehan. "She's cute. No hardship having a partner that looks like that, right?"

I watched her and remembered why I had liked her. That made me smile. "When we chew the cud and remember the old times, Jane, it won't be in an interview room. Maybe we can catch up later. But right now we are here because you have evidence relating to a murder inquiry."

She sighed heavily and looked down at the table. She was slim and shapely. Her face was pretty, nice to look at, but her eyes, which were a dark, rich blue, made her somehow more than just pretty. They gave her an odd, captivating beauty.

"All right, Mr. Detective, we'll do it by the book. Yes, I have fresh evidence relating to Kate's murder. You look great, by the way. Time has been kind to you."

"Thank you. I appreciate that. What is the nature of this evidence, exactly?"

She looked at Dehan, sighed again, and shook her head. "You been stuck with him long?"

"A while."

"It turns out that while Kate was my personal assistant, I was receiving letters from someone who might have been a stalker. They started out nice enough, but as time passed and I didn't answer him, they became more"—she paused to think of the word, then said, "intense is I guess the word."

Dehan was frowning and making notes. "Were they threatening? Did they threaten you with violence at any time?"

"Not exactly. I don't think so, anyway. Kate lived at home with me. Danny and I have a very large house, and we found it was just easier if Kate lived in with us. She had no private life to speak of, and this way, she enjoyed a level of comfort and luxury she could never aspire to otherwise.

"As my personal assistant, I trusted her absolutely, and she used to take care of my mail. As you can imagine, I get a lot of fan mail as well as crazy mail, and she would take care of it, filter out the irrelevant, and make sure I got the stuff I did need to see."

I said, "And she never told you about this stalker."

"No. When she was..." She took a deep breath. "When she passed on, for a long time, I couldn't bear to go in her room or look at her stuff. I loved her dearly as a member of the family. But recently, a couple of weeks ago, I started going through her stuff and deciding what to do with it. She had no family except us."

Dehan said, "And you found the letters?"

"There were all sorts. Some she had dealt with, others were waiting to be read and either thrown away or answered or filed. And I found those, all signed, 'Your Man.'"

"Any idea why she kept them?"

"No." She gave her head a small shake. "I can only think that she assumed he was a harmless nut, but something about him made her uncomfortable. She was a very sensible, grounded person, and maybe she thought we might need the letters to get a restraining order if he started parking across the road."

I asked her, "Did you bring them with you?"

She reached down beside her and came up with a plastic grocery bag which she handed to me across the table. "I don't think that's all of them. There seem to be some missing. And there are passages here and there that make me wonder if she got into correspondence with him."

"Like?"

She pulled a folded piece of paper from her purse and smiled at me as she handed it over.

"I've done enough cop shows and movies to know that evidence should be touched as little as possible. When I realized what these letters might be, I made a list of the passages I thought were significant and sealed the letters in a plastic bag. The only prints on the letters should be Kate's, mine, and the writer's."

Dehan nodded. "Good job."

I looked at the list. There were a series of quotes, and beside each quote was a date and two numbers. Jane pointed at them. "The date on the stamp, the paragraph, and the line. I haven't read everything. Like I said, when I realized what they might represent, I sealed them up."

I scanned through them, then read out loud, "'I'd like you to look me in the eye and tell me that,' 'You are standing between two people who were destined for each other. That will have bad consequences.' 'God made something beautiful, and now you are making it foul.'"

Dehan reached across and pointed to a quote near the bottom and read out loud, "'I know you are lying.' That's about as close as you can get to conclusive. If he considered it a lie, she told him something. They were having some kind of a dialogue."

Jane nodded. "That's what I thought."

I folded the paper and put it in the bag with the letters. Dehan leaned out and called a name. A moment later, the door opened and a sergeant came in. I handed her the bag and told her, "Get these copied, then send them to the lab. Label them Jane Morley, the case is Katy Hagan. Tell Joe I'll call him."

She said, "Will do" and left. I turned back to Jane.

"Is there anything else? Did any of this bring back any kind of memories? Did any conversations or comments, any change in her behavior, anything at all come to mind?"

"No, but then I haven't really given it any thought, John. I found these, started reading them, and contacted you."

Dehan asked, "Who takes care of your correspondence now, Jane?"

"I have a secretary."

"Did you ask her if you had continued to receive similar letters after Kate's death?"

"Yes." She nodded. "Of course, it was one of the first things I did. She said she had never seen anything like them and told me I should go immediately to the police. Which I had already decided to do."

I nodded. "Okay, Jane, give us a couple of days. We need to go through these with a fine-tooth comb and have the lab look at them too. After that, we'll be in touch and let you know how things are progressing. Meantime, if you think of anything, just call me or Dehan."

I handed her my card. Dehan slipped hers across the table. "Any developments, keep us posted."

I stood and opened the door for her. She paused a moment to look at me, then smiled. "Thank you, John. It was nice to see you again."

And she walked out.

CHAPTER 2

We spent the rest of the morning working through the letters, reading them. Things that stood out were the fact that the letters were typed on an old-fashioned typewriter, but, as Dehan pointed out, the address on the envelope was handwritten in neat, elegant script. To add to the apparent inconsistency of those facts, the signature, 'Your Man,' was also typed.

Dehan scratched her head and left a few loops of hair standing up. They made her look cute and were hard to ignore. "Is he stupid," she said, "or is he trying too hard to be smart?"

I shook my head for a bit, then shrugged. "He got somebody else to write the address and post them. We'll probably find an extra set of prints on the envelope."

The content of the letters started out pretty inoffensive but seemed to build in paranoia and narcissism as the letters progressed, particularly when the first suggestions of a dialogue with Kate started to emerge. After a while, I dropped the letter I was reading on the desk and crossed my arms.

"Imagine for a moment you get a serious crush on Hugh Jackman."

"This is before I met you, right?"

"Thank you."

"Otherwise it's just too hard. You know, when you've been with the best..."

"Is this about sticking with the four-bedroom house in Maine plan?"

She smiled and blinked.

"Okay, so you develop a big crush on Hugh Jackman, and you decide to send him a fan latter." She snorted. I ignored her and went on. "You don't know at this stage that you are shortly going to becoming a paranoid narcissist and kill his personal assistant. You're just writing him a nice fan letter telling him how cool he is, right?"

"Okay."

"So why would you type the letter?"

"Maybe I have really ugly handwriting. Maybe I am dyslexic."

"That could make sense, but it raises three more questions. First, who types these days? If you want to send a physical letter instead of an e-mail, you print it. Who has a typewriter? Also, is that why you signed it 'Your Woman' instead of using your name?"

She grunted. "That is odd. If it was just one or the other, you could dismiss it, but all together, it suggests he already knew he wanted to hide his identity."

I nodded. "I think it does. Okay, let's get this stuff to the lab. If we are just a little bit lucky, this guy might have a record for stalking or sexual offenses, and we might just find him on IAFIS."

Dehan gave the look of skepticism. "When he has taken care to type the letters, sign with a pseudonym, and get somebody else to address the envelope? I don't think so, Sensei. But we gotta check, right?"

I made a *whatcha gonna do* face, and we headed out for the Jag, shouldering on our jackets.

We took the Bronx River Parkway as far as the zoo interchange and then turned east onto the Pelham Parkway. It took a little less than an hour, and by midmorning, we were sitting with Joe in his makeshift office drinking coffee from paper cups amid teetering stacks of reports. While we sipped, he examined the letters and the envelopes one by one.

"So let me see if I've got this straight. He types the letters on an old typewriter, he signs with a typed pseudonym and then either writes the addresses by hand or gets somebody else to do it for him."

Dehan answered, "That's what it looks like."

"So I have an observation and a question. My observation is that typewriters are, in principle at least, easier to identify than printers, because of the idiosyncrasies of the keys. My question is, having gone to the trouble of typing the letters, why didn't he type the envelopes? Surely that would be less trouble, and less risky, than involving a third person by getting them to handwrite them."

I nodded. "It had crossed my mind. If he'd used a printer, you might explain it because for dinosaurs like me, lining up the labels or the envelopes can be a pain. But this is a typewriter. You roll it in and you type."

He didn't look at me. He was staring at the letters and the envelopes, which he had set out side by side. He said, "Yes" in an absent kind of voice.

"You seen something?"

"It may be nothing."

"But it might be something. What is it?"

He raised his shoulders an eighth of an inch. "The envelopes are the kind of thing your aunt in Maine might use. Heavy duty paper, blue with a tiny white fleck. You wouldn't be surprised if they were scented with lavender."

Dehan made a "Huh!" sound.

He went on, "The paper is good quality but nothing special. And his prose—" He shook his head. "It's kind of dry, unfeeling, even when he gets mad. It's totally at odds with the envelopes."

"So he used his mother's envelopes but not the letter paper because it had pictures of kittens on it, or…"

I interrupted, "Letter after letter, for over a year?"

"Or," she went on, "this guy sees himself as subtle and smart and leaves lots of red herrings that lead nowhere."

Joe sighed and sat back. "There could be a million and one explanations. Let's see what we get from the fingerprints. If they don't lead anywhere, it might be worth taking these to an FBI profiler. There are a number of striking incongruities. It's not a lot to go on, but sometimes they can be very helpful."

I asked, "How long will the prints take?"

"Lifting the prints is pretty quick these days; the rest is up to the software. I might have something for you later this morning, but I can't promise."

We finished our coffee, made our way down to the parking lot, and strolled toward the Jag. Dehan linked her arm in mine, and I watched my feet. There was a chill in the air.

"Incongruities," I said.

We stopped by the car, and I looked for a moment at two or three brown leaves that had settled on the grass. The fall was coming.

"Was the killing itself incongruous, Dehan?"

"Yes."

I rested my ass against the door and studied her face. Her cheeks were flushed with the chill, and her eyes were bright. "What was incongruous about it?"

She shoved her hands in her coat pocket and went up on her toes. "The location, the apparent rage of the killer toward an apparent stranger, and the fact that Kate was there at all."

I opened the car door for her, slammed it when she'd climbed in, and went around the hood to climb behind the wheel. There I sat for a moment staring at the tree with its two dead leaves at its roots.

"So let's try a little thought experiment. A big, brutal guy beats Kate up, breaks a few bones, and stabs her several times. For the sake of the thought experiment, we will say that the guy is Jane's fan who has turned out to be a psychotic narcissist. His rage is caused by the fact that Kate will not mediate between him and Jane. So he has persuaded her, we don't know how at this stage, to meet with him. There, in a fit of rage, he beats her and stabs her to death for the purpose of removing the obstacle standing between him and his love, Jane." I paused and spread my hands. "And having done that, he vanishes into thin air and stops stalking her." I nodded for a bit at the tree. "That for me is the most incongruous thing of all. It is even more incongruous than the sensible, grounded Kate agreeing to meet him in the first place." I turned to look at Dehan. "But Joe is right. There are a lot of incongruous features to this case. Everything is wrong, and there ain't nothin' right."

She waited a moment, then added, "I agree, and I know you're getting at something, but I don't know what."

I made the face of ironic humor and eyed her a moment. "Well, if you find out, let me know, will ya?"

She snorted a humorless laugh. "So what now? Maybe we should go talk to Danny Santos. He might know something without knowing it, fresh perspective." She looked out the window, pursed her lips, and spoke with a voice that would have made sandpaper look moist. "She struck me as a woman who thinks she knows everything but misses the subtle nuances."

"Subtle nuances, huh? She struck you that way?"

"Uh-huh." She eyed me. "What? I can't say subtle nuances? All the time I gotta be the Latina for you, papito? What about my soul? What about my personal growth?" She looked away. "I have subtle nuances too, you know?"

I sighed and pulled out of the parking lot, shaking my head quietly to myself. I was heading for the Morris Park exit when my cell rang. I saw it was Joe and pulled over to answer.

"John, where are you?"

"By the Rose Kennedy building, why?"

"You're not going to believe this. We got a hit."

"On IAFIS? So soon?"

"It was very recently added to the system. He's a multiple offender. I'm emailing you the details now."

I thanked him, and a moment later, my cell pinged. I handed it to Dehan. "We got a hit already. Multiple offender, recently added to the database."

She watched me pull out and head for Morris Park again. I glanced at my phone in her hand and then at her face.

"What's the matter? Who is he? What's his name? Where does he live?"

"I can't read and ride, Stone. It makes me seasick. I thought you knew that."

"Sure." I raised both hands. "My bad, I should have realized. We'll stop at Emilio's for ice cream pizza with waffles and Branston Pickle."

"Don't pick on me. And don't tell me I've got hormones or I'll kick your ass all the way to Texas."

We drove in silence for a couple of minutes. Then she sniggered. "You heard about—this is my dad, right? You heard about the Jewish guy who tells his wife they should spice up their sex life?"

"Nope."

She had a sheepish grin on her face that made me laugh. "She asks him, 'Spice it how, Irah? What kind a spice? What you want me to do?' He says, 'Mira, you could moan. When we are making love, you could moan.' 'Moan? You want me to moan?' 'Yeah,' he says. 'You could moan sometimes.' So next time they're makin' it, right? He's givin' it all he's got, and she says, 'Irah, should I moan?' He says, 'No, not yet!' a few seconds later, 'Irah, should I moan yet?' 'No, not yet! Not yet!' 'Irah, should I moan now?' 'Yes!' he says, 'Now! Moan now!' So she starts, 'Such a morning I've had! I couldn't sleep all night with the pain in my knee...'"

She doubled up with her hand on my shoulder, emitting a high-pitched laugh. I pulled in and parked outside Emilio's as she leaned back, flapping a hand at me. She clung to my arm as we crossed the sidewalk and leaned her head on my shoulder with tears in her eyes.

"God I miss my dad, Stone. He would have loved to see our baby."

I pulled her chair out for her and kissed her head as she sat. I sat opposite. "I know, honey, it's tough. You know I'm here for you anytime you want to talk or—"

"Yeah, thanks, Stone. That's sweet. Means a lot. Listen to me. His name is Bob Newport. He has several convictions going back fifteen years, uh...indecent exposure, soliciting a prostitute, groping a female police officer..." She chuckled, then frowned. "No, that's bad, a police officer should not have to encounter the commission of crimes while performing her duties, right?"

"Dehan."

"Yes?"

"Are you okay?"

"Sure. He lives at 1026 C, Faile Street, in Longwood. Unemployed."

"This guy could be dangerous. You want me to drop you at the station?"

Tears welled in her eyes. "You really care about us, don't you? Me and baby."

I smiled. "Of course I do."

"I'm being stupid. I know. I'll wait in the car. I'm your partner, and I should go in with you, but I should not expose him—her—to risk, right? Maybe you should get another partner."

I was spared having to answer by Emilio ambling over. I ordered a beer, and Dehan had a green tea. When he was gone, I said, "Listen. The absolute most important responsibility you have now is to look after yourself and the safety and well-being of our baby. You want to stay here with Emilio, you want to go home, to the station or stay in the car, it's all good with me."

"I'll stay in the car."

"If I think he's inoffensive, I'll give you the nod, and you come on in."

"Okay, thanks, Stone."

She looked away, and I pretended to be interested in the grain in the wood on the tabletop. Hormones can be contagious.

CHAPTER 3

It was a bare brick 1930s construction with three floors plus a basement. Each of those floors had a bow window, which gave the impression of a castle tower running up the side of the house. When it was built in the early part of last century, it was probably a nice family home, with the kitchen and the help in the basement. Now it was four apartments with an old TV and a washing machine decaying on the sidewalk.

I parked in front of the house and climbed the six steps to the porch and pressed the bell labeled C. Behind me, I heard my car door slam. I turned and saw Dehan standing at the foot of the steps. She shrugged as an electronic voice crackled from the door.

"Yes?" It was a high, thin voice. It didn't sound like the Hulk on steroids.

"Mr. Newport? Bob Newport?"

"Yes, who is this please?"

"My name is Detective John Stone from the New York Police Department. I wonder if you could spare me ten minutes."

There was a long moment of silence, then, "What's it about?"

I sighed audibly. "It's about Jane Morley, sir. I'd rather not have this conversation on the doorstep, and I'm pretty sure you don't want that either. Do you think I could come inside?"

The door buzzed, and as I pushed it open, I was aware of Dehan by my side. She shrugged again as she squeezed past me. "He doesn't sound dangerous, does he?"

"No, but neither did Ted Bundy. Just stay behind me and let me talk to him." Her face told me I was about to get a mouthful, so I added, "*Both* of you!"

She pressed her lips closed and let me climb the stairs ahead of her.

We reached apartment C on the third floor, and I rang the bell. The door opened a couple of inches, and beyond the chain, I saw a small face peering out at me.

"Can I see some ID, please?"

I showed him my badge, and Dehan showed him hers. "I am Detective Stone, this is Detective Carmen Dehan, NYPD, from the 43rd precinct. May we come in and talk to you?"

I saw his eyes fix on Dehan, and after a moment, he closed the door and opened it again without the chain to let us in.

We were in a small passage. On the left was an open door which led to a large room with a bow window overlooking Faile Street. We followed him in. There was a sofa and two armchairs that didn't match. They were old and shabby and had that air of having been bought from a thrift store. There was also a coffee table and a TV, a table by the window with two bentwood chairs, and little else.

He stood beside the sofa. He was maybe five ten, more out of shape than overweight, late thirties with abundant dark hair. He spoke suddenly.

"Should I make coffee? I don't—people don't—I don't see people. Often. I don't know. Sit down?"

I smiled. "That's okay, Mr. Newport. We had coffee already. May we sit?"

I took an armchair, and Dehan took the other. Bob perched on the edge of the arm of the sofa with his hands clasped between his knees.

"You wrote some letters—"

"I write lots of letters. It's a thing I do. I don't work, but I read a lot, and I write a lot of letters. That's not a crime now, is it?"

He straightened with mild indignation as he spoke, but his small hands were still between his knees. I watched his face. His cheeks had colored slightly, and his eyes were bright.

"No, Mr. Newport, it is not a crime to write letters. May I finish what I was going to say?"

"Sorry. I'm a bit quick off the mark. It's the dyspraxia. DCD, developmental coordination disorder. It makes me anticipate, and usually I am right. I'm not clumsy. I seem clumsy, but I'm not. Sorry..."

When he was done, I smiled again. "No problem. The letters I am talking about you wrote a few years back to Jane Morley. Do you remember that?"

"Yes, you said over the intercom. Wonderful actress. I was desperately in love with her. So warm, and those *eyes!* My God." He sighed.

I leaned back in the chair and crossed my legs. I wasn't sure what I had expected, but this sure as hell wasn't it. "Do you remember the correspondence you had?"

"Good Lord, it was years ago! Must be ten years? Maybe more. And it was hardly correspondence. *I* wrote to *her*. She never wrote back."

"Have you some idea of how many—"

"I think maybe I got on her nerves. I have a range of disorders, you know, and in some cases, I can't hold my focus. If people are too slow, or they take too long to get where I *know* they are going, I lose focus. *Too* slow! *Too* slow!" He laughed and slid off the arm of the sofa onto the seat. "But other times, my focus is *huge,* and I can stay focused for hours, days, even weeks, and that is the only thing I can focus on. So you know, I might have written her a whole barrage of letters and not even realized it."

"You don't remember?"

"Do you remember the letters you wrote ten years ago?" He

turned to Dehan. "Do you remember the letter *you* wrote ten years ago?" He gave his head a little shake. "My goodness, you are *beautiful*. You have that glow—" He stopped dead, and his jaw dropped open. "Oh my God!" And then again with more emphasis, "Oh my *God!*" He glanced at me, and in a fraction of a second he had read my face. He clasped his bottom lip with his teeth and smiled.

"Mr. Newport, can we stay on task please? Did anybody from Jane Morley's team ever write back to you? Maybe to ask you to send fewer letters?"

He still had a goofy grin on his face. He gave his head a small shake. "No."

"You never received a message from Kate Hagan, Jane Morley's personal assistant?"

He gave a small laugh, like it was only slightly amusing how hard it was for people to keep up. "So we'll climb back *down* the ladder of abstraction. I think I just answered that question. I never received a message from Jane's team, which includes her personal assistant—about anything."

I sat frowning at him, momentarily unsure which way to go. He took a deep breath that said he was being more patient than I deserved.

"Detective Stone, I fell in love with Jane Morley some ten years ago or more. My various conditions make me a very focused, passionate person at times. Most people despise focus and passion. I wrote to her and bared my heart. I sent her poetry and opened my very soul to her, but either she never received my letters or, as you suggest, her personal assistant *made sure* she never got them. Equally likely is that her agent, Henry Silva, kept them from her, or forbad her to answer. After all, he would not want to share control of his little treasure, would he?"

I gave my head a small shake. "No."

I sat forward with my elbows on my knees. My neurons were engaged in a small riot in my head, and I was having trouble thinking.

"Bob, Mr. Newport, I might want to talk to you again. Do you have a cell where I can call you?"

He heaved another sigh. "But you will please delete it as soon as the case is closed."

"Sure."

He gave me his number and accompanied us to the door. All the way, Dehan was frowning at me like I had started speaking in tongues. But she didn't say anything until we were in the car and I was staring at the bare trees that lined the road. Then she said, "What the hell was that about?"

"I don't know."

"You were done with him? I thought you were just getting started."

"He wasn't what I expected." I turned and frowned at her face. "Incongruous," I said. "I felt like I'd been dropped in the middle of Beijing with a map of Paris."

"I hope you're not being careful on my account, Stone."

"Don't go there, Dehan. That's not it. He was learning more about us and the investigation than we were learning about him." I looked at her again. "He picked up that you were pregnant *and* that I was the father, just by reading us. I was not ready for him, and I was not going into a fight I didn't know how to win."

She was quiet for a moment. "Yeah, he picked that up real fast. So what do we do now?"

"Besides," I added as an afterthought, "I got the feeling he was telling the truth." I sighed. "Now? We go back to the station, get some lunch, and read those letters again. And maybe, maybe make a visit to Henry Silva this afternoon."

She watched me fit the key in the ignition, but before I turned it, she said, "You don't think it was him, do you?"

I turned the key, and the engine roared.

"I don't think anything right now, Dehan. But it did strike me that he is a foot shorter than he ought to be, and the only bones he is liable to break if he hits anyone are the ones in his hands, and the only brutal attack I see him pulling off is the one against the creases in his pillow."

She shrugged as I pulled away. "I hear you, but you and I both know that rage can not only change a person, but give them strength you'd never expect."

"Ritoo Glasshopper speak wisdom words. But Big Stupid Sensei need to regroup and think."

When we got back, Dehan walked down to the deli, and I sat and read through some of the letters again, some from the beginning, some from the middle, and some of the last ones he had written. The phrasing of the earliest ones was recognizable as Bob Newport. It was affected and camp, and left no doubt that he 'adored'—his word not mine—Jane. But as the letters went by and he got no response, the style seemed to change. I sat and scratched my head, staring at one particular line.

...YOUR FAILURE TO RESPOND, even to my most sincere, heartfelt revelations of my own feelings for you, speak of a cold, callous lack of emotion which I never dreamed you would be capable of...

I WAS STILL STARING at it when Dehan came in and put my two roast beef sandwiches and large coffee in front of me. I said, "Listen" and read the short paragraph that followed those lines:

"'Or does it speak of something else? Does it speak of the parasites and carrion-eaters that surround you and imprison you, and insulate you from my words, depriving you of your freedom —and my love? What do they fear? I ask myself, who is reading these words, if not you? Whoever it is, I ask them now, what do you fear?'" I looked up at her. "Does that sound to you like Bob Newport?"

She sat and opened her sandwich. "No." She bit into it, and as she chewed, she asked, "What are you getting at?"

"Is this a case of multiple personality disorder? You read through these letters, and he changes. He starts out as the Bob Newport we met this morning, but he gradually changes. His way of writing changes. He becomes..." I spread my hands and shrugged. "There is only one way to say it. He becomes more *masculine*. I mean, let's face it, if we didn't know that he was obsessed with Jane Morley, we would both have assumed he was not just gay but camp with it. And that's the way he writes in his first letters, like he's writing to Judy Garland. But over the space of a few letters, he becomes increasingly masculine. Is it a dual personality?"

"Jeez, boss, you're in deep water now. I have no idea." We stared at each other while I unwrapped my sandwich and bit into it. Then she said, "Are you serious or just being provocative?"

"I don't know." I swallowed, drank coffee, and asked, "But you know what I've been thinking? I've been thinking that Bob Newport, with his various disorders and phenomenal capacity for focusing his attention, must have an exceptional amount of information on Jane Morley and the people in her inner circle. Did *you* know who her agent was before he told us? I didn't." She grunted, chewed, and watched me. After a moment, I asked, "Do we know what he looks like, Henry Silva? Is he big, powerfully built? Is he as possessive as Bob wants us to believe?"

She chewed, shook her head, and spoke with her mouth full. "Djonow. Lesh foinjow."

Scan the QR code below to purchase CURTAIN CALL.
Or go to: righthouse.com/curtain-call

Printed in Dunstable, United Kingdom